Desperate Measures

Published by Martin Singer and Sleep Writer Publishing
Cover design by: Rebecca Covers
Edited by: Heidi Thomas
Proofread and consulting services by Sandra Starkey

Printed in the United States of America

Desperate Measures

Martin Singer

1

Tessa Holland sat on the floor in the corner of their upstairs bedroom, eyes swollen, legs pulled up against her chest. She crumpled another tissue and added it to the pile scattered on the floor around her. Pain wrapped its icy fingers around her heart.

Snippets of her conversation with Dr. Johanson spiraled through her mind. "Troublesome first pregnancy." "...further tests." Dread erased all the gynecologist's reassuring words.

The sound of gravel crunching on the driveway signaled her husband Ray's arrival. The back kitchen entry door opened, followed by the sound of shuffling feet and keys clashing on the counter.

I should go down. He'll want to eat. Tessa dug deep within to find the energy to get to her feet. She'd made taco casserole with Doritos, a favorite of Ray's and left it sitting cold on the counter.

Another long day at work as an engineer at Laubner Labs. Tessa had grown used to the frequent late night meal preparations, but this night was important. *How will he react? Will he be angry? Upset?*

"Tessa?" he bellowed.

The time had come. Time to bring him up to date on the serious nature of their situation - the most important thing in their lives today. Standing at the top of their narrow stairwell, her body tensed, recalling the conversation about the need for a handrail before the pregnancy progressed too far along. Placing her hand on the wall, she stepped carefully down each creaking step, every one adding to her annoyance. Reaching the hall landing, she paused.

Ray stretched his arms, yawned, and offered a half smile. "Sorry I'm late."

"Again." She pushed past him into the kitchen and picked the cold casserole off the counter.

He touched her arm. "Don't worry about that."

"What, this? Your favorite. I cooked it special for tonight." She gazed down at it, wondering how this was to change their situation. She'd had such high hopes, the meal to be a celebration of good news, maybe entice Ray to take time off to help her along in the pregnancy. She let out a loud sigh.

But no, nothing was according to her plans.

Ray positioned himself in front of her to take charge of his own belated dinner. Just as he reached out to grasp it, she released her grip. The dish plummeted to the floor, shattering into pieces, spraying reddish Dorito chips, tomato sauce, avocado chunks, and sour cream onto his slacks and dress shoes.

"Was that really necessary?" He scoffed. "I said I was sorry." He stepped back, assessing the damage.

Without looking at him, she growled, "I thought maybe you would be interested in my visit with the doctor today, but no, apparently it's not important to you."

The phone rang. They both jumped but continued to stare at each other, waiting for the other to make a move toward the phone. Ray broke the stillness, raised both arms high above his head, and snapped, "I'll get it."

"I bet it's your mother." Tessa sighed and shuffled out of the kitchen into the privacy of their living room. Debra Holland always seemed to pick the most profound times to call. At times, even sober. She could understand keeping tabs on her only child, but sometimes two calls per day felt intrusive. As soon as her in-laws knew she was pregnant with their first child, the calls had become regular, full of advice.

#

Ray whipped the receiver from the wall mounted phone. "Hello."

Sobs and garbled words broke through the line.

He frowned. "Mom, slow down, get a hold of yourself. What's going on? Have you been drinking?"

"Dad f-fell. H-he's on the floor."

"Wait, what? Is he breathing?" Ray rubbed his left hand across his forehead, trying to soften a sudden sting of pain above his left eye.

More sobs.

"Mom, call 911. Hang up and call 911."

"Oh my gosh, what do I do? Help me!"

"Mom, hang up and call now." Ray disconnected, then dialed 911.

He gave the dispatcher his parents' address, including all he knew of the circumstances. She wasted no time in dispatching a medic unit while keeping Ray on the phone. Tapping his foot against the floor, he waited until they finally confirmed his mother's presence on the line. He hung up after providing his cell number so they could reach him in transit.

He yelled to Tessa, "We need to go, right now."

She hurried into the kitchen, her emerald-green eyes red and swollen, a crumpled tissue in her hand. She sniffled. "What's going on?"

"That was Mom. Dad collapsed." He frantically scanned the kitchen for the car keys. "I called 911 for her. They'll call me with an update, but we need to head to Stanford Hospital. That's where they'll take him."

She stepped out of the kitchen, grabbing her coat and purse, and brushed at dark wet spots on her blouse. "Let's go."

Ray followed behind her out the kitchen door onto the concrete carport where one of their two Subarus sat parked.

#

Tessa placed both hands on her shoulder belt to ease the swaying as they raced down Route 84 at twenty over the limit. Ray's cell phone rang. He answered, hit the speaker button, and tried to hold his phone steady while bouncing along the rough road. The urban Palo Alto landscape was only a blur in the early evening darkness. A calm female dispatcher explained that Ray's father had a heart attack and was on the way to Stanford Hospital, as he expected. His mother was with him in transit. Ray thanked her and disconnected the call. With both hands gripping the steering wheel, he pushed the accelerator to the floorboard.

Tessa gripped the sides of her seat. The tires squealed, breaking loose on a turn. She yelled, "Ray, slow down...please. Getting there sooner won't change your father's situation."

"My father may be dead if we get there too late," Ray thundered.

"Ray, please, slow down. Please, for the baby's sake," she pleaded.

"My father...and now you drag the baby into this." He sneered, his face red.

He slammed his right foot hard on the brake pedal. The Subaru's tires squealed and came to a sudden stop.

Tessa held her breath and placed both hands on her bulging middle to support the five-month-old fetus from smashing into her abdominal wall. The stench of burning rubber and hot iron filled the car as it sat idle in the center of the darkening road.

Ray's knuckles were white, gripping the steering wheel, his head resting in its center, breathing hard. Tessa turned her bowed head, her long brown hair strands partially obscuring her view. A tear fell onto her blue jeans.

"Ray, you're going to get us all killed." She whimpered as she drew back a batch of hair. "We've talked about this. This erratic behavior has to stop. Too often, you're not thinking things through. Viktor could have killed us both months ago, when he kidnapped me and you dumped the FBI Agents. The GG-2 launch – you'd be dead if I didn't rescue you. And GG-1 –"

"Stop, enough... enough. I can't change the past." He slapped his hands on the steering wheel.

"I know that, but you need to get a grip, slow down, carefully plan your...our lives and these projects. These past several months, you've seemed so distant."

"I get it, I get it," he grumbled.

"Do you, Ray? Are you sure? You didn't even ask me what the gynecologist said about the baby today." She flipped her hair away from her face, sat up straight, and stared at him.

"Is that why you started into me when I walked in the door? Why you were upset?"

"Yes," she whispered. Another tear ran down her cheek. She swiftly wiped it away. "There's a problem with the — Watch out!" she screamed.

Everything plunged into darkness.

2

Ray opened his eyes, unable to move his arms and legs as he rocked back and forth to the movement of the dimly-lit white space. A muffled siren wailed. A shadowed form leaned over him and shined a bright light in each eye, forcing them open wider with rubber gloved fingertips. His left ankle throbbed, and he had a metallic taste on his tongue. Muscles twinged with each breath.

A radio emitted a crackling sound, and a woman's voice spoke. "This is Aid ninety-four. We are inbound with a twenty-four-year-old semi-conscious male, involved in a two-vehicle collision in which his car was struck from behind by a large van. Airbags were deployed. Due to extensive damage, the roof was cut away to get to the patient. Initial vital signs BP one-sixty over eighty, pulse ninety, respiratory rate twenty, skin pale, and diaphoretic. Left ankle is bruised and swollen. Left chest is bruised. Patient is secured to a backboard, c-collar on and a splint has been applied to left ankle. Our ETA is five minutes."

Ray groaned. "What happened? Where's Tessa?"

"He's conscious," the same voice spoke. "Can you hear me? Can you tell me your name?"

"Ray, Ray Holland," he whispered, as each word caused wincing pain in his chest.

"Do you know what day it is?"

Ray moaned as his body rolled from a hard turn, the belts pressing against his soreness.

"Friday, August twenty-fourth." He grunted.

The young attendant, dressed in her blue cotton shirt and pants, grabbed a stainless-steel bar to fight the centrifugal force of another hard turn taken by her driver.

"Ray, you've been in a car accident. Do you know what happened?"

"Tessa, where's Tessa?"

"Was Tessa the other passenger in your car? Do you remember what happened?" The attendant leaned in close.

"Yes." Ray recalled the conversation, the explosion of glass, metal, then nothing. He forced out more words. "My... father? Heart... attack... On our way... to see him."

"I don't know about your father. Were they taking him to Stanford Hospital?"

"Yes." A renewed worry overwhelmed him concerning his mother's actions in the ER. What if she had been drinking? How would they handle that in the hospital? His mother wouldn't be someone to just tell to go lie down and sleep it off while Dad's life lay in the hands of an emergency room doctor. With no other siblings to deal with her, he was alone, now partially incapacitated himself.

And Tessa. What about the baby? What news would she have received? Was that why she was furious when he arrived home? Or was it not being with her at the appointment? He couldn't help that they were performing the first test of the new fusion laser that day. Laubner Labs, his employer, required an "all engineers on deck" for the event. At least this time, firing the fusion laser went without a key failure. The results remained disappointing, forcing his team back to work on Monday. He bet they expected him there, despite his injuries.

The ambulance doors snapped open, a rush of cool air flushing in, the sky a dark contrast to the brightness of the emergency room entrance. The gurney snapped; a sharp stinging interrupted any further thoughts. The straps crushed his chest. Voices shouted his status: "Stable, BP one-sixty over eighty, pulse ninety, respiration twenty, possible fractured left ankle, chest bruising. Take him to room three."

"Where's Tessa?" He groaned into the oxygen mask over his mouth to no one apparently listening.

3

Dimitri Mishkin stared through the floor-to-ceiling window of his luxury Moscow apartment at the Moskva River, reflecting the few lights illuminated at early dusk. His heavy frame sank deep in his favorite dark brown leather chair, and he tipped back his shot glass of cognac. The chair was an admired piece he'd stolen from a dock office in San Francisco years earlier and transported on one of his aging bulk carrier merchant ships, the *Arisha*.

The merchant trade was much softer now with the new Russia and more competition, although his trading in goods of a secret nature remained the most profitable. In the United States, the San Francisco Bay Area held many prospects, including a favorite US defense contractor, Laubner Labs in Palo Alto. Excelling at bribes and navigating the American system, he had profited handsomely until he unfortunately was caught and expelled from the country permanently.

Dimitri grasped the half empty bottle of cognac and poured another shot. He swirled it around, gazing out the window to the laughter of younger voices. He stood, stepped over to the view two stories down at a scattering of young men and women. Some were pushing strollers, some walking with toddlers. Two groups of young men and women together, likely out for a night of fun. He had hoped to be a grandfather by this time, but it had not happened. Tipping back the cognac, he thought of his own children, his two grown boys.

To Viktor, his oldest, he taught the trade. It proved to be difficult. His ability to read prospective company insiders came especially hard. Then, once on the FBI or Central Intelligence Agency watch list, he had to go underground and disappear. Viktor didn't do well trying to be invisible, frequently turning to brute force to accomplish his tasks. Dimitri knew this wouldn't go well for his son, so when the news came from the Russian State Department of his death, sadly, it came as no surprise.

What came as a surprise was his death wasn't at the hands of the FBI or CIA, but he was found dead by the FBI. Some sort of unexplained explosion, that was all he knew. Their last conversation months earlier mentioned a brilliant young engineer at Laubner, a Ray Holland, moonlighting on some sort of energy device that he felt would be sellable on the black market. Maybe this Holland would know more about what happened to his Viktor. He doubted Holland would know why the State Department held the body so long before releasing it to next of kin. Upon the release he wired $10,000 US dollars to have the body shipped to Moscow for a proper burial next to his wife, who died three years earlier after being struck by a car.

Dimitri's younger son by three years, Vladislav Mishkin, took the news of his brother's death particularly hard. Currently, he served as a first officer on the *Arisha*, which had recently departed the Port of Tacoma in Washington State after delivering Diammonium phosphate. Choosing to head for the San Francisco Bay Area and wanting to save on the cost to ship the body, Vladislav insisted on retrieving his brother. Dimitri refused, wanting to close this chapter of his life sooner than the month it would take *Arisha* to arrive at a Russian port.

Vladislav shared in his father's grief, also wanting to know more about how Viktor died, or who was responsible. Dimitri, although sympathetic, felt it a waste of time dealing with the US State

Department on such matters. Mentioning this Holland person from Laubner was all he could offer his sorrowful son in search of answers. Finishing the rest of his Cognac, he sighed, feeling an emptiness he couldn't understand.

4

Doctor Stevenson stood at the nurse's station in blue scrubs, a stethoscope dangling from his neck, reading a clipboard of their next expected patient. Leaning against the counter, he sighed and wiped his thick glasses, dirty from the long shift.

He'd seen his share of car accident victims over his ten years as an ER doctor at Stanford Hospital. Swiping his black, medium-length hair back off his ears with his free hand, he mentally prepared for the soon expected arrival: a twenty-five-year-old pregnant female, removed from a serious two car accident thirty minutes earlier. Cuts to her head, vaginal bleeding, bruising, swollen arm, unconscious. Vitals noted BP eighty over fifty, pulse eighty but irregular, breathing twenty and shallow. Ray Holland, her husband, arriving fifteen minutes earlier, was stable in room three.

Directing his attention to the nurse at the station, he asked, "Do we know when the other car accident patient will arrive?"

"Another ten minutes, I think they said."

"Why the delay?"

"Her being pregnant and something about having to restrain the other driver, apparent DUI. He was trying to help the paramedics, said he was a former navy seal. They said he's handcuffed in the back of a patrol car now."

"Room one stat when she arrives."

"Yes, Doctor."

Stevenson quickly jotted a few notes on the clipboard before heading toward room five. His earlier patient who had suffered a heart attack was unresponsive when they arrived. He sighed heavily. Twenty minutes of chest compressions, six defibrillator jolts, epi and Amiodarone, intubation, all for naught in this case. The first of the Hollands arriving, a strike three in terms of tragedy for the family this night. A hospital case worker sat next to Mrs. Holland, who was sipping coffee to sober up.

"How's she doing?" he asked.

The young lady stood, stepped close and whispered, "She appears to be coming around, although she breaks into some serious crying."

"Okay. We're going to need this room soon, so could you move her to one of the bereavement rooms? Her son is in room three, a car accident patient. But it's too early to take her to see him."

Shouts erupted from outside the room.

"That's my other accident patient. I'll catch up with Mrs. Holland as soon as I can."

Dr. Stevenson ran toward Room one, a flurry of paramedics and ER nurses crowding around a speeding gurney headed his way.

The young, slender female paramedic shouted out the vitals again. Little difference from the earlier report. Tessa Holland's slim-fitting blue jeans, blue blouse, bra, and pink panties were all cut off in the exam room. Her socks were last to go, revealing a recent pedicure with pink polish and a toe ring on her left big toe.

Stevenson noticed the small baby bulge and dark clotted blood pooling between her legs. Not a good sign. Her skin pale, still unconscious, blood pressure low.

"Start a couple units of blood stat," he ordered while moving to the head of the exam table.

A dark reflective plastic bag soon dangled on a stainless-steel pole, attached to an IV line already in place. The scurrying, masked, gowned team completed hooking up ventilator, automated blood pressure cuff, and pulse monitor on her finger. After the vigorous activity settled, Stevenson moved around, placed a stethoscope to her chest, and listened.

"Lungs sound clear." He moved down to her belly and listened. As he could only make out his patient's own soft heart beats, he called for an ultrasound. Concerned about the vaginal bleeding, he understood normally he would hear the baby's heartbeat with a stethoscope at the estimated twenty weeks. The fetus could be farther along than the baby bump showed. He gently removed the splint from her left arm and asked the staff to order a mobile X-ray unit. After palpating her abdomen, he leaned in and checked her pupils with a penlight. They responded normally.

"Mrs. Holland, can you hear me? I'm Doctor Stevenson. You're in the emergency room at Stanford Hospital. Mrs. Holland, if you can hear me, squeeze my finger." He placed his finger into her palm. She didn't move. He checked inside each ear next — both pink, a good sign of no significant head injury. Reaching gently under her head, he checked the neck vertebrae, satisfied with the alignment. Remaining concerned about the unborn fetus, he asked the team to call up an OBGYN doctor stat. Intently watching the monitor, he breathed a sigh of relief that her vitals were stable. Knowing his team would keep a close eye on Tessa, he walked the short distance to room three to speak with her husband.

# # #

As a doctor stepped through the beige plastic curtain into room three, Ray tried to sit up, groaning from the chest pain. "Where's Tessa, my wife? Is she here yet?"

"Easy does it, son. I'm Dr. Stevenson." He put a hand on Ray's arm. "Lean back and relax. Tessa is here, two beds down the hall."

Fear clutched his heart. "How is she? Is she okay?"

"Mr. Holland, we have a lot to go over. Sit back and try to relax." Stevenson waited while Ray lay back, grimaced, and then breathed a sigh after another muscle spasm sting.

"First, your wife is stable, but hasn't regained consciousness. She has a bruised left arm, and we're trying to find the status of her baby."

"Oh my God, this is all my fault," Ray moaned as his muscles spasmed in his chest and back again.

"Mr. Holland, we need to talk about your father. He came into the ER as well. Your mother is here. I'm afraid I need to let you know when your father arrived, he experienced a major heart event. I'm sorry. Despite our attempts, we couldn't restart his heart."

The shock hit him like an electrifying jolt. The same as when he touched Uncle Bob's hot-wire cattle fence as a child. Ray's mouth opened, but he couldn't speak. Tears ran down his cheeks.

"Mr. Holland, your mother is here and is understandably upset. She's in one of the bereavement rooms with our care staff. We can bring her here to see you if you like."

He whispered, "Yes." Turning his head to the wall, he wept. Dr. Stevenson stood still for a moment, then left the room.

#

The case worker gently guided Debra Holland into room three. She held a tissue to her wet, swollen eyes.

When she saw Ray in the bed, she stood taller and cried out, "Ray...Ray, your father is dead. He's dead, Ray. Why did this happen?" She stood motionless for a moment and stared at her son lying there, hooked up to tubes and monitors, and her eyes welled up again. "Ray, why are you in bed?"

"Mom, we were in an accident on our way to the hospital."

"Are you hurt?"

The case worker placed a padded metal chair behind her and gently helped her sit.

"Mom, what happened with Dad?"

Furrowing her brow, she glanced around the windowless room. "I told you, he's dead. Weren't you listening?"

"Mom, no, I mean, how did this happen? Was he exercising?"

She glanced at her feet searching for the memory. "We were in the living room together after dinner. He was reading the paper in his leather chair by the window when the phone rang. It was Laubner calling. Glen, I think his name is. His boss." She sniffled and dabbed her eyes, remembering. Anyway, your father's face turned red while on the call, then he scolded Glen, telling him it wasn't true. Those were his exact words. Then he slammed the phone down."

She swallowed around a lump in her throat. "I asked him what that was all about, and he just said, 'work stuff.' He got up, walked into the kitchen. I heard the water turn on, then he went into the den. I heard something, thought it was the neighbor working on his big truck again. When your father didn't come back, I went to check and found him on the floor. That's when I called you."

# # #

Ray knew Glen was more than just his father's direct supervisor; he was the VP of operations in the fusion and powers systems division at Laubner. Not someone to speak harshly to or just hang up on. This guy answered directly to the board of directors. What had he said to upset his father so much? He had to know.

5

The emergency room filled with a high-pitched chirping as a young nurse in blue scrubs, blonde hair, and glasses rushed to room 302. The pulse monitor on the small black screen showed a flat white line. The nurse spotted right away that her patient Tessa Holland was breathing, her blood pressure slightly elevated from the last hour. Looking at the pulse oximeter on her fingertip monitoring her heartbeat, she realized it had slid off.

Placing it back onto her finger, she spoke to Tessa. "That thing is so loud, I don't know how you can stand it. We have to come check for every little alarm."

She checked the IV line and her freshly-bandaged, severely bruised arm. Unfortunately, according to her chart, her baby had aborted. An obstetrician team took charge and completed the procedure to assure Tessa experienced no further blood loss. After she completed her checks, she headed back to the nurse's station, but as she stepped out of the room, the chirping wailed again.

Returning, she could see the monitor was off Tessa's finger again, but she couldn't locate it. Moving closer, she found it gripped tightly in the woman's hand. Silencing the monitor, she looked at Tessa's face, noticing a twitch of her eyebrows, then a slight roll of her head. She pressed the call button, and the nurse at the station answered, "Yes?"

"Hi, this is Tracy. Tessa is stirring. Can you let Dr. Stevenson know?"

Moments later, Stevenson pulled the curtain aside and stepped in. "Is our sleeping beauty waking up?"

Tracy filled him in on what had taken place. Dr. Stevenson placed his finger in her hand and asked her to squeeze.

"Okay, you can let go now. That has to be the strongest grip I've felt in quite some time." Pulling his finger away, he asked, "Tessa, can you wiggle your toes?" Nurse Tracy pulled the sheets back. The toes on both feet wiggled.

Tessa's eyes remained closed. Dr. Stevenson explained to Tessa where she was, that she had been in a car accident, her husband was alive, and had sustained a broken ankle and some cracked ribs. Tessa shifted her hand to her stomach, and soon her breathing grew labored.

"I'm sorry, Tessa, but your baby was stillborn."

She slowly opened her eyes, as her breaths continued deep and labored. Nurse Tracy's eyes welled up, and her lips quivered as she witnessed Tessa's response.

Stevenson placed his hand on her chest. "Tessa, try to slow down your breathing. I know this is tragic news."

Tessa glanced back and forth between them and gently asked, "Was I able to hold my baby?"

Stevenson said, "I'm afraid I don't know the answer to that. She's in the hospital morgue at this time."

"She? A...girl? My baby's...a girl?"

"Yes, she was a girl. I'm sorry for your loss."

Heavy tears ran down the sides of her face. Nurse Tracy dabbed them dry, then placed the tissue in Tessa's free hand, holding it there for a long moment.

Tessa whimpered. "Will I be able to see her?"

"Of course. You and your husband can see her as soon as you're both able to walk down to the morgue."

"My husband, does he know yet?"

"Yes, he was quite upset as well."

Tessa gazed at the ceiling panels, her eyes resembling heavy raindrops on fresh wax as she looked at Dr. Stevenson, then at Tracy, inquiring, "When will I be able to see my husband?"

"He's getting discharged today. He has a cast on his left foot because of a fractured ankle, and three cracked ribs, so he won't be doing too much moving around. He'll be eager to come see you awake now."

"What happens now with my baby?"

He pulled up a chair and seated himself next to Tessa.

"Your husband signed off on the certificate of stillbirth, and a burial permit."

"What? I don't understand. What about my opinion?"

Stevenson let out a quiet sigh. "Unfortunately, you were in a coma."

"Wait. What name is on the death certificate?"

Stevenson glanced at his watch and looked at Tracy, pressing his lips together firmly.

"I'm afraid I don't know." He stood from the chair at her bedside. "Your husband is more aware of these details. You will need to speak with him."

"Where is my husband?" she snarled.

"I'll go see if they discharged him." Stevenson faced Tessa from the end of her bed. "I recommend you try to take it easy to help your body heal. Again, I'm sorry for your loss." He then moved toward the open door.

Nurse Tracy snugly tucked the sheets over Tessa. "Now you heard the doctor, please relax. If you need anything, you let me know."

"I want to see my husband."

6

A clunk sounded as the wheel bumped against the door frame of room 302. The tall male nurse pushing the wheelchair announced, "Someone is here to see you."

From the wheelchair, Ray ran a hand over his hair. *Probably in desperate need of a comb.* He smiled, seeing Tessa awake for the first time in days.

Ray opened his mouth, but Tessa spoke first. "Our baby is dead, Ray. Our baby girl is dead."

"Yes, I know. I'm so sorry."

"Are you sorry, Ray? Sorry enough to care?" Her voice rose. "Sorry enough to listen to your wife when you drive too fast? Sorry enough to consider my opinion when it comes to our life together?"

Ray held up his left hand. "Wait, stop. I said I was sorry. I cared enough to take care of you and the baby while you were in a coma."

"Wait, what? What do you mean, take care of the baby? The baby is dead, Ray."

"There's paperwork. Decisions to make."

"What decisions?"

"I know it sounds morbid, but they said she wasn't old enough for a formal burial. Our baby is being cremated.

The nurse stood up straight, let go of the handles of the wheelchair, and slowly stepped back. "I'll be back in a few minutes."

"You were in a coma, Tessa. These things can't wait." He winced as he placed his hand on his chest.

"Well, I'm awake now, so we can make these decisions together," she shouted. "First, I want to see our baby girl."

"I'm not sure that's a good idea."

"What do you mean? If I want to see my baby. I get to see my baby."

"Tessa, the baby was twenty weeks old. The doctor ordered an autopsy."

She turned her head away. "This is your fault, all your fault." She took a long pause before speaking again. Giving him a bold stare, she growled, "Please leave."

"You want me to leave?"

"Yes, Ray. Leave now before I do something, something I may regret."

Ray stared, his mouth a rigid frown. His chest ached inside and out like never before. A tear ran down his cheek and fell to his bare arm. Taking a deep breath, he said, "If it's any consolation, my father is dead too. Mom went home bawling and is probably sitting in the kitchen drinking away her sorrow. I'm in no position to help, being her only crippled son. I've had a loss too."

Tears continued to stream down his cheeks as he grabbed the wheels of his chair and backed out of the room.

Outside her room he paused, contemplating his next move. Disgusted with himself and his miserable situation, he wheeled to the nurse's station and made arrangements to go home.

7

Angelina Nikitin and Vladislav Mishkin stood on the deck of the merchant ship *Arisha*, scanning out into the fog that had settled into the Southern San Francisco Bay. Vladislav smiled, looking through the binoculars for his associate to arrive on his twenty-nine-foot rigid inflatable.

Angelina ran her fingers through her damp hair. "This fog is messing with my hair, Vlad."

"Quiet," he scolded. "I need to listen for Mikail Sokolov to come, take us to shore. This fog is good for us, so no one sees us depart."

"Don't the Americans have radar?"

"Quiet."

A faint motor idling like the purr of a cat echoed off the *Arisha*'s hull. Vladislav pressed the button atop the air horn, sounding three short bursts. Angelina covered her ears, then scowled at him. A moment later, a white boat emerged from the haze, cautiously approaching the side of the ship. Vlad signaled the crew to lower the gangway so he and Angelina could disembark.

Unfortunately, the gangway would not completely reach the skiff, leaving at least an eight-foot gap. Angelina stepped to the end of the gangway first and noticed the dilemma. She turned to face Vladislav. "Now what?"

"Jump. But don't fall in."

She glanced down at the distance and turned to face him again.

"Just jump." He tipped his head in the direction of the skiff.

Squatting, she then sat on the end of the plank, her legs dangling over the boat in constant motion with the sea. With a firm grip on the edge, she patiently waited for the boat to be directly beneath her before propelling herself forward. As she landed on the soft cushions at the bow of the boat, she lost her balance for a moment and accidentally bumped into the side of the inflatable rubber vessel. Throwing up her arm at her success, she glanced up at Vladislav as he stood waiting.

"Are you coming?" She placed her hands on her hips.

"Yes, yes." He waited a moment, then jumped. He landed with a thud, his legs rigid, which made him stumble backwards. He reached out, placing his hand on the *Arisha*'s cold steel hull to steady himself and avoid falling into the icy bay.

Mikail smiled at the successful landings, shook hands with them, and then embraced Vladislav.

"How far to the dock?" Vladislav asked.

"In the fog, to be safe, maybe two hours. If the fog clears, much sooner. It's a public place close to Palo Alto where you said you need to go. Bair Island Marina. No one will notice us. You can call for a rental car."

"Good. This is Angelina." Vladislav gestured toward her.

She scanned the boat for a place to sit. Mikail reached up with his hand, tipped his Oakland A's baseball cap, and smiled.

He reached his hand to Vladislav, holding his business card from the consulate. "Here. Address you wanted is on the back. When you want to return, just call me. I will pick you up."

Vladislav glanced at it, then placed it into his inside jacket pocket.

He and Angelina sat behind the pilot seat of the boat as Mikail accelerated south in the dense fog. Angelina tucked her long hair into her jacket, and they sat in silence as the powerful Mercury engine roared behind them.

#

Arriving at the Bair Island Marina an hour and a half later, the mist had cleared from the water and the sun illuminated a bright sky. They stepped onto the dock, thanked Mikail, and waved goodbye.

A ship horn's blare interrupted the squawking seagulls fighting over a crab carcass on the cracking concrete floating dock. Angelina pinched her nose. The intense odor of creosoted pier poles nearby filled the lingering damp San Francisco Bay morning.

"What's the matter?" Vladislav asked as they walked toward the parking lot, waiting for the arrival of the rental they ordered. Angelina brushed at a wrinkle in her slim fit blue cotton jeans.

"Maybe ship's bad smell has ruined my nose. I am ready to see American perfume store to cover this up," Angelina said, trying to speak better English while in America.

"In time, in time. We must first find this Ray Holland."

"Why is this so important? I want to shop in America and replace this blouse. It smells of the ship and is so old." She brushed at a rusty brown stain on her shoulder.

"This Ray may know how my brother died."

"Your brother was evil. How many has he killed?"

He turned and grasped her shoulders, jerked her close to his face, and snarled, "My brother is my blood. He does what he is told. You could stand to do the same, or maybe something may happen to you."

Ready to spit in his face for roughing her up, she held it, and smiled. "Why would you hurt me, threaten me? We are a couple. What? A year now? I came with you on this long journey. We have sex. You should be happy with me."

He released his powerful grip and patted her shoulders. "Sorry." He glanced around. "Don't speak badly of my brother. My father loved him, made rich by many of his works. Now my father expects more from me. This is troubling for me. I must find out what happened to Viktor."

He grabbed her hand and continued to walk toward the parking lot.

8

Ray winced, sliding out of the yellow cab idling in his driveway. He set his crutches on the ground, and attempted to stand with his weight on one foot. Reluctantly, he tipped the driver, who simply sat, eager to get to his next fare.

Glancing at his New England gray painted garage door, which appeared tightly closed, he recalled when he and Tessa returned home from the Vegas trip. The door was open, his personal GG-1 project and powerful-fusion formed stones gone, stolen.

The powerful stones were a byproduct of a fusion test failure many years before, gifted to him by his father. He'd been greeted by the FBI who were more interested in catching the killer of two of their own than his stolen project. He snorted. If they knew the history, they'd be more concerned, but the FBI was not the attention his project needed. With a limited quantity of fusion stones remaining, it would hamper his research into their powers.

He had downsized his original designs from the one which flew supersonic across the Bay Area, the other having created a deep hole in the desert. He was hopeful to produce a final design that could yield new leads in fusion power research and recognition for his achievement.

He gingerly placed a foot on the single step of his side entry, and then entered the back door. Needing a couple of ibuprofens for his chest and throbbing ankle, he wished he had a cure for the pain deeper in his chest. *Why does this hurt so much?* Tessa, the baby, his father. He was so alone. Should he call to see if she was still upset, or just sink into his favorite leather chair, close his eyes, and hope for an answer? His cell phone rang.

"Mom," he answered.

"Ray, are you still in the hospital?"

"No, I just made it home."

"Oh good. Can you come over and help me go through your dad's belongings? Every time I walk into the closet, I start crying."

"Mom, has the funeral home called you to make arrangements?"

"Yes, but I'm just not ready, so I hung up. Can you do this for me?"

Holding his breath, he winced then sighed. Having already messed up his baby girl's arrangements, now he needed to help with his father's. *Maybe this will help...or maybe not.* He didn't want to sulk in the corner.

"Give me the number, and I'll take care of it. As long as you agree whatever I choose to do, you won't complain. Now try to relax and remember the pleasant things about Dad. I'll be over this afternoon."

"That would be great. Can you pick up a bottle of Chablis? I'm almost out."

"Mom, you need to take it easy on your drinking. We have lots to get to, and you need a clear head."

"Honey, don't worry about me, it's only wine. It's not like I'm drinking the stuff your father drinks when he gets home from work."

Ray had heard enough. He recalled the conversation about Laubner and how upset his father was with the call from Glen, the VP of operations. His father was a responsible engineer, and he had passed up several promotions to stay lead in his group, a team he knew well, and had grown to love. They played golf together in Palm Springs twice a year, all with serious handicaps. Someone had to buy drinks at the end. Ray smiled, knowing his father likely paid for several rounds. But why get so upset with Glen?

"Mom, I have to go. I'll see you this afternoon."

He ended the call.

# # #

A knock came from the direction of the front porch door. *Now what?* Door to door sales in his remote neighborhood? How stupid that would be.

"I'm coming," he shouted as he took long steps with his crutches and opened the door. A man and a woman stood out front, not dressed all that well, but the man looked familiar...too familiar. An image burned into his mind from several months before. *Viktor Mishkin.* But he was dead, and this man looked younger, somewhat slimmer, the face remarkably similar.

"Are you Holland, Ray Holland?" he asked with a strong Russian accent.

"Yes, who are you?"

The man pushed the door open and strode past. Ray grabbed the doorjamb to prevent his collapse to the floor. The attractive younger blonde woman followed, a confused expression on her face.

"What are you doing? You can't come in here like this!" Ray hopped on his good foot to face his unwelcome guests, the door still wide open. "What do you want?"

"Ah, Mr. Holland, that is a question I will answer." The stocky man with short blonde hair paused, swiveling his head, examining the house and its furnishings. Placing a finger to his chin, he said, "I need to know of my brother, how he died?"

"Oh, no." Ray asked what he already knew. "You're Viktor Mishkin's brother?"

"Yes, yes, of course. This is Angelina, I am Vladislav."

"How did you find me?"

"Find you? I have many associates here in America, so very easy. Now, my question. What happened to my brother?"

He puffed out his chest. "I'm not going to answer any of your questions. You're trespassing, and you both need to leave before I call the police."

Vladislav reached his hand behind his back, pulled out a Glock 17, dark and shiny, now pointed at his chest.

"You will answer, or maybe join my brother."

He felt his stomach collapse. His eyes locked onto the gun. There was no way to escape. Not with his foot in a cast, his good leg now burning.

"I need to sit down." He still held the front door jamb for support.

"Of course, shut door and sit, we talk. We have much to talk about."

Angelina pulled a wooden chair from the kitchen and set it behind Ray, allowing him to sit. She carefully removed his crutches from his grasp. Vladislav frowned and rolled his eyes, still standing, the gun now pointed at the floor.

"So, you know how my brother died?"

Ray held out his hands, palms up. "A tragic accident is what the FBI told me."

"Mr. Holland, I believe you know more than your FBI."

Ray glared at the gun in the man's hand. "Viktor kidnapped my wife."

"Viktor maybe misguided at time. Is your wife pretty? Maybe he wanted a girlfriend."

"He kidnapped her, called me, and wanted me to do a demonstration." His chest burned at the memory.

"A demonstration. Demonstration of what?" Vladislav scratched an apparent itch on his temple with the barrel of the Glock 17. Ray watched carefully, hoping the gun would fire and eliminate half of this duo.

Vladislav brought the gun down and pointed it at Ray's chest.

Ray gulped. Can I lie my way out of this, get these two out of my messed-up life?

"It was a project. A device that can fly."

"Like a plane?" The Russian paused. "Why would Viktor be interested in a plane?"

"No, nothing like that. It had no wings. It levitated."

"What do you mean, levitated?" He waved the gun around.

Angelina interrupted, standing close to Vladislav. "I know levitate. It floats like bubbles in air."

The man turned his head and frowned. "What? I know some American words." He held his finger to his lips.

Angelina scowled, her face flushed a rich shade of red.

"Angelina, maybe you should look around while I talk to Mr. Holland alone."

Angelina pushed away from the leather chair she leaned against and glanced toward the office-like den, the kitchen, then at the stairwell.

"Go upstairs." Vladislav pointed with the Glock.

"What? I thought you were here for information, not to rob us," Ray spouted.

"Mr. Holland, rob you? No. Angelina needs a, let's say, distraction."

Angelina bounded up the creaking stairway. Ray glared. If Tessa knew a stranger was snooping around, she would freak out.

Vladislav stepped closer.

"What happened to you?" He pointed his Glock at Ray's cast and crutches.

"Car accident."

"You seem to be in some pain."

"Yes."

"Pain is a powerful tool, you know, Mr. Holland."

Ray sat up straight, squirmed, then winced.

"Let me show."

Vladislav lifted his left leg, placed his boot on Ray's cast foot, the Glock still pointed at his chest. He pressed down. Ray winced, trying to pull away, but Vladislav pressed harder. Ray groaned.

"Now, maybe you know more of my brother?"

Ray just moaned, his face beginning to heat.

Vladislav removed his foot and peered at Ray's chest.

Ray looked up at his face and frowned.

Vladislav leaned in with his free hand fisted and punched Ray's chest. He screamed.

"Ah, that's better." Vladislav smiled. "Now I have your attention?"

Ray remained stoic, his mouth firmly closed, knowing the truth would only bring more pain.

A shout came from upstairs. "Vlad, what is going on?"

"Nothing that concerns you."

Vladislav swung his Glock against Ray's head.

Ray screamed again and collapsed to the floor.

"Mr. Holland, I am more patient than my brother. You should tell me what I want."

Lying on the floor, Ray held a hand to his temple. His fingers came away blotched a rich red.

"My project killed your brother. It launched and struck him."

Angelina scrambled down the stairs, a pink blouse in her hand, clinking with glass objects wrapped inside.

"What the hell, Vlad? Enough. You said you would not hurt him."

Angelina approached Vladislav. He placed his hand on her chest and pushed her back. She lost her balance, thumped to the hardwood floor, and landed flat on her ass. The blouse with glass contents landed softly in her lap, saved from hitting the hardwood.

Reaching back with his free hand, preparing to strike her, Vlad stopped, then laughed.

"Angelina, you best keep still, quiet." He turned to face Ray who still lay on the floor gripping his bleeding temple. Angelina rolled onto her hip, then her knees, stood, and glared at Vladislav while he focused on Ray.

She turned and walked toward the den.

"So, Mr. Holland. Did you watch this happen?"

"Yes." Ray groaned, glaring at the blood on his hand.

"Did you not warn my brother?"

He held out a clenched fist. "No. Your brother is a murderer and kidnapper of my wife. He would have killed us, so…"

"So, you killed him," Vladislav interrupted.

"Him or us. I chose him." Ray spat between clenched teeth.

"Mr. Holland, you know we Russians are traditional. Eye for eye, we say. I should kill you now."

"No," howled Angelina, standing in the den doorway.

"Quiet," Vladislav snarled as he pointed the Glock at Angelina. "Mr. Holland, I am afraid we need to take a trip, as my father will want to avenge his loss, personally."

"I'm not going anywhere. There's no way you'll get me on a plane at gunpoint, and as soon as I protest at the airport, you'll be arrested."

"Ah, this is where you are wrong, Mr. Holland. We will go by sea on my father's ship. Security is, let's say, not so strong at the port. So, putting you on board will be easy. But I put you in a box if I have to."

Ray relaxed his neck, resting his head on the floor as he stared blankly at Vladislav's feet. What more could go wrong in his life? *Tessa, the baby, now I'll die for trying to save my and Tessa's lives.* Tormented, his heart was broken...*take me now.* At least they would find his body here, bury it next to his father, and there would be a new manhunt for his killer.

"Why don't you just kill me now?" Ray wasn't sure why he spoke the words.

"I would be happy to, but my father would be most upset. Where is your wife? You wouldn't want her to come home to your bloody corpse, would you?"

"She's in the hospital. Probably wishing I was dead."

Vladislav raised the Glock to his temple, scratching his apparent itch again. "So, bringing her along may be more trouble than it's worth. My father might take her as a special prize to relieve his pain though. He only has me now. My mother gone three years. It would please him to lay with a woman again."

Angelina walked out of the den with a round shiny metal donut-shaped dish-like object in her hands. Brilliant blue-green, fluorescent marble-like stones glowed inside. "These are very beautiful." She held it out, showing it to Ray, smiling. "These look very expensive. How much you pay for these?"

Vladislav examined the stones and their container. "Hmm, yes Mr. Holland, how much you pay for these?"

"They were a gift."

"Maybe we will have more to bring to father, help pay to fix *Arisha*. Are there more?"

Ray glanced between the two, raised his chin higher, a slight curve on his lips. "In the garage."

Angelina set the device on the oak coffee table next to the blouse containing the items she'd removed from the bathroom upstairs. Turning toward the back door, she pointed, questioning the direction.

Vladislav held up his hand. "You stay here with Holland. I will go see garage."

As Vladislav left the room, Angelina strolled into the kitchen, opened the freezer, and grabbed a handful of ice cubes. She placed them in a hand towel hanging on a bar nearby. Ray watched from the floor, leaning on his forearm. Angelina approached and reached out her free hand toward him. After wiping the blood onto his pants, he grasped her forearm. She tenderly guided him to a seated position on the floor, cradling his head and applying the iced towel to the swollen bleeding knot. Ray winced, although the coldness relieved some of the hot pain.

"Vlad should not have hit you," Angelina whispered, kneeling, her hand still cradling the back of his head.

"I would have preferred that." Ray focused his glance into her bright blue eyes. "Since we're on the subject, I would prefer not to die, either."

"Mr. Holland, how much can we sell stones for?"

"I don't know. I've never tried to sell them."

"I know Vlad's ship needs much repair. I want to go to university. My mother dead many years, and my father has no money, only a small farm. My two sisters work the streets of Moscow for food. A shameful, violent job. When I met Vlad, he saved me from this."

Ray raised the back of his hand, delicately stroking the lightly swollen pink cheek on Angelina's face. "I think you haven't been spared from some of his violence."

Angelina's face flushed.

"I don't understand Vlad, why he angers. He has given me many pretty things; says he can't afford university. I think I may be just a, let's say, sex toy maybe. He teases the *Arisha* crew, has me wear tight clothes since I am only woman on board."

Angelina lifted his chin, adjusted his posture, then guided him back to the wooden chair.

"You are very pretty, Angelina. I understand his attraction to you. I don't understand the physical violence men take against women."

"Is your wife pretty?" Now standing, she straddled one leg, facing him.

"She is, but she hates me now."

"Why would she hate you? You are a good-looking, rich American man." She pointed around the room full of furniture.

"She blames me for losing our baby." He lowered the towel to his lap, staring at it. Fresh pain rose from his gut.

"Your baby died? That is so sad." She frowned then placed her hand on her stomach, rubbing. "I want a baby, but Vlad says no baby for us."

Ray looked up as she stood tall over him, her long blonde hair tangled. He wasn't sure what to say.

"Do you have American passport?" Angelina asked.

"Yes. Why?"

"Was it for your job?"

"It was a job requirement."

"Where is it?"

"In my desk." Ray pointed to the den office off the living room.

She walked past him, and he watched her slide a heavy oak desk center drawer open in the office. Lifting the folder and opening it, she removed two blue passports, and put the folder back in place.

"This is your wife?" She held the open passport toward Ray.

"Yes."

"She has pretty eyes."

"Angelina," came a shout from the back kitchen door. "*Idi pomogi mne.*"

Shoving the two passports into her back jeans pocket, she hurried out, leaving Ray alone.

9

The door jamb shattered as Vladislav put his heavy leather boot against the dark green-painted door. He toggled two switches located by the entrance, causing the fluorescent lights to flicker momentarily before gradually illuminating the room. Two plastic gallon buckets rested on an old, dark paint-peeled table. Poster sized mechanical drawings and cardboard tube containers lay nearby. Smiling, he gazed inside the buckets at what could be an abundance of value his father would be proud of.

A couple more machined metal donut-shaped objects rested on the table with black boxes, stringy wires protruding. A dark plastic reel containing shiny copper wire rested on the floor. Not familiar with electrical engineering, he frowned. The drawings were a mystery. Growing up in his father's shipping business, the greasy, dirty work of hydraulics and diesel were all he really understood. He'd obtained all the RYA and ICC training and licensing to captain the *Arisha*, but he didn't want the responsibility. He wondered about the drawings, what they meant.

Was this a device like the one that killed his brother Viktor? The drawings printed in English didn't help his understanding. He would have to ask. Under the table he noticed a much larger metal object, with mesh screens, wires coming out of the center, and more of the stones scattered inside. He attempted to shift it to get a better view, but realized it was too cumbersome to handle alone.

Vladislav stepped outside and shouted for Angelina. Then he went back in and tried to slide the large, shiny object across the floor.

"*Vlad, gde ty.*"

When he heard Angelian's voice, he stood, waved his hand, and pointed at the buckets and metal objects on the table. He explained in Russian that it all was going into the car and to the *Arisha*. She shrugged. They loaded the trunk full and put the remaining two buckets of fluorescent stones into the back seat of the rental.

He led the way back through the kitchen door, stepping into the living room. Ray sat in the chair with a wet towel. Vladislav stared, then swiveled his head, examining the distance between the kitchen and where Ray sat.

"How did you...?" He glanced at Angelina. She smiled. He rolled his eyes, shook his head.

"Mr. Holland, please explain the objects in your garage."

Ray sneered. "I'm a dead man. Why would I tell you anything at this point?"

"You're not dead yet." Vladislav stroked his chin with his finger and thumb. "Maybe your wife knows."

Ray snapped back, "Leave her alone. She has nothing to do with any of this."

"You say she is still in hospital? *Arisha* is in no rush. We can wait."

"Leave her alone," Ray growled.

Vladislav turned to face Angelina. "Help Mr. Holland to the car, we should go."

10

Tessa awakened at Dr. Stevenson's voice. "Knock knock."

He slid the heavy glass door in room 302 to the side, followed by Sophia, the floor nurse assigned to her.

"How are you feeling?" The tall doctor stood next to the hospital bed.

I would love to cry for my baby until every last drop fell from my face. To scream until everyone heard my anguish. To shake sense into my husband, wherever he is. "That's a tough question. Do you have a few minutes?"

He smiled. "Let's start with your arm."

"Less sore since taking the Percocet." She glanced at her left forearm, wrapped tightly in gauze.

"It should heal quickly since it's just a nasty bruise, and you're young. I have good news. We can release you this afternoon. You'll need your husband or other family member to drive you."

"Well, I've been unable to reach my husband, so my parents will be my ride. They should be here any time. They just arrived in town from a vacation in Europe."

"We need to review your discharge instructions, which Sophia will go over with you, but I want to go over the results of the fetal exam."

Shouts came from the hallway. Tessa recognized the voice. "That's my mom."

A woman scrambled into the room, wearing a loose, button-up blouse with an imprint of the Eiffel tower, beige slacks, and flat shoes. Gasping for breath, she shouted, "Tessa, oh my God, are you all right? We found your message on the house phone and caught the next available flight. Is the baby okay?"

Tessa scanned the doorway. "Where's Dad?"

"Chuck is parking the car. He'll be here in a minute. But I need to know —"

Dr. Stevenson interrupted. "I'll come back in a few minutes."

"No," Tessa insisted. "I want to know what the report says. My parents can hear this too. This is my mother, Natalie Holmes."

"Hear what?" Mom asked. "Does this have to do with your baby?"

Sophia handed a clipboard containing several pages to Dr. Stevenson, and he flipped a couple sheets.

"It was determined the girl was twenty-two weeks, based on size and development of her..."

"Was?" Her mom's her face went pale. "Our grandbaby is dead?" She collapsed to the floor. Nurse Sophia, too late to stop the fall, quickly knelt to evaluate Tessa's mom. Tessa pressed her head back against the pillow, and gazed up at the ceiling, biting her lip to keep from crying. *I knew she would take this hard. Her hopes were off the chart looking forward to the baby.*

Dr. Stevenson stepped around the bed and pressed the call button to the nurse's station.

"Do you need something?" the female voice called.

"This is Stevenson. We need help with a visitor who passed out."

"Right away, Doctor."

A page announced for help stat in room 302. Tessa leaned forward, glanced down at her mother, then laid back, placing her hand to her forehead.

"Is she all right? I can't get up, my head is spinning."

Soon a male nurse better suited for football than nurse care stepped in, knelt down to help lift the groggy Natalie from the floor. Another nurse walked in carrying a wooden chair and placed it in the room. They lifted her, one on each side, and carefully seated her. Another nurse held out a paper cup full of water. Dad stood nearby, a puzzled look on his face.

"Doctor Stevenson, please continue," Tessa insisted seeing that her mom was awake and sipping water.

"As I was saying, the fetus was twenty-two weeks, based on cranial development, weight, and length. No visible signs of trauma or defects upon external exam. But the internal examination showed both heart and lungs were underdeveloped for a fetus of this estimated age. A lung lesion was discovered, weighing sixteen ounces. Preliminary indication of Fetal Pleural effusion. Right lung and ventricle —"

"Doctor Stevenson," Tessa interrupted. "I wish I could understand the details of the entire report, but the more you read, the more confused and nauseous I'm feeling. What I need to know is, did the baby die because of the car accident?"

"Simple answer, no. Didn't your gynecologist go over the last ultrasound with you?"

"She did. I needed to discuss the options with my husband before we considered the risky surgery."

"I'm afraid, based on what I read here, surgery would not have saved the fetus. If it hadn't aborted after the accident, you would have lost it within the next couple weeks." His face softened. "I'm sorry again for your loss."

Tessa glared at the doctor. "I need to call my husband... I've made a terrible mistake."

11

Stopping at the end of the Holland driveway, Vladislav put the rental in park and gazed at Angelina sitting next to him.

"We have a problem."

She shifted in her seat and sat up straight. "Getting all of this on *Arisha*?"

"Yes. I need to talk with Mikail. He will know, so you drive."

They stepped out of the car and switched places, then she pulled out. Vladislav removed his cell phone from his pocket and dialed.

"Mikail, this is Vlad. I have problem for you."

"Yes, I can probably help."

"I have some cargo, and a special guest to get onto *Arisha*. The gangway will not work using your boat."

"I have a bigger boat," Mikail offered.

"My special guest has a foot injury."

"Oh, I see. Your ship has a crane, yes?"

"Yes." Vlad cocked his head.

"I have some crates we can use for the cargo, maybe your guest also. We would need to go to my home. Would take less than one hour from marina."

"Good. I have one other request. My special guest has a wife who needs to come with us, but she is in hospital."

"Leave her alone," Ray shouted from the back seat.

Vladislav pulled out his Glock, turned, and smashed it across Ray's temple. He toppled to the floor, lying unconscious on top of the buckets of fusion stones. Angelina stared at Vladislav, her mouth open, but remained silent. She looked over her shoulder at the unconscious Ray, his temple bleeding.

"Sorry," Vladislav apologized after placing the phone back to his ear. "That was my special guest."

"I understand. What is wife's name?"

"Tessa Holland."

"Which hospital?"

"I don't know and can't ask now."

"No problem. We have access to all their databases at the consulate. I have a particular vehicle just for these types of occasions. But you must do me one favor."

"Yes. Yes, of course."

"There are two special guests of mine at my home. Young guests. You must mention to no one."

Vladislav gazed at Angelina, furrowed his brow, and ran the pistol across his mouth, suspecting she'd overheard the request. Angelina pressed her lips together and gave a slight nod.

"We understand."

"And your guest, I have proper head wear for him. He will see nothing but the dock."

"If you come soon, he will still be asleep."

"Good. I will see you in one hour at marina."

12

The homes along the San Leandro Bay varied from fancy wrought iron-fenced and luxurious to weather worn and run down. Many owners couldn't keep up with property tax payments, so enhancements to the properties were infrequent. All the houses sat twenty to forty feet apart, most of which with extensive overgrown shrubs offering ample privacy for those that desired it.

Mikail found this extremely valuable for the activities at his leased property. Operating under the company name of Campus Youth Administrative Services, thwarted the inquiries that had come in regarding activities on the property. The quiet waterway also provided covert access throughout the San Francisco Bay Area, compared to the busy Fernside Boulevard in front of the home. The residence south of Mikail's was one of the local vacancies and had been for the last two years. On the northern side lived an elderly couple, but they never ventured outside, and aid cars frequently visited them.

Mikail steered the rigid inflatable toward the concrete floating dock. Ray lay unconscious, a black hood over his head, on the cushion-covered bow of the boat, along with the GG devices and stones. An hour earlier, while at the marina, there were a few too many people mingling about, even one boater that offered to help carry items to the boat.

Vladislav requested Angelina charm the man so they could be undisturbed, so she asked questions about the man's boat, which he eagerly provided, including a tour. When he asked why they were carrying Ray to the boat, she told him he was seasick. When asked about the blood on his head, she described it as a fall. He asked no further questions but seemed eager to show this attractive foreigner with an accent his thirty-two-foot Catalina sailboat from bow to stern.

Mikail leaped from the rigid inflatable onto one of two of his large floating docks, held in place by four concrete pilings. He swiftly tied off two lines. Vlad stepped off, then reached back to help Angelina off the boat.

At the other dock was a forty-foot modified tugboat painted bright orange and white. Mikail pointed. "We can use this boat for the transfer. It was a pilot boat, retired after many years of service."

Angelina smiled at the larger vessel with an enclosed cabin, which appeared much more stable than the rigid inflatable she had just stepped off.

"We can transfer everything here on the docks. No one will notice or pay any attention as long as your guest remains asleep," Mikail instructed. Angelina glanced back at Ray, who still lay motionless on the bow of the rigid inflatable. "Come, I will show you the crates we can use."

Vladislav gazed at Angelina. "You stay here, keep an eye on Mr. Holland so he doesn't fall overboard and drown. It's not time for him to die quite yet."

Mikail and Vladislav carried a large crate and placed it on the dock next to the rigid inflatable. Vladislav instructed Angelina to set the buckets of stones and smaller items into the crate, while still keeping an eye on Ray.

As the two walked back toward the house, Mikail noticed the girls at the door and waved his arm signaling them to move away.

One of the girls boldly made a hand gesture, but both turned and moved back into the darkness.

The second wood crate they set on the dock was about the size of a coffin and included a lid. They moved it toward the edge of the dock, next to the rigid inflatable, before stepping onboard.

Mikail lifted Ray over his shoulders while Vladislav held the boat steady against the dock. He dropped Ray into the box like a bag of potatoes, his head slamming against the plywood bottom. They secured the top on the crate, hiding its human contents before heading to retrieve the last box. This one was large enough to hold the larger GG device. With a cordless drill, Mikail drilled air holes into Ray's crate and inserted wood screws to hold the lid in place. Using a hoist on the modified tugboat, they soon had all three crates loaded on the stern of the vessel.

Vladislav and Mikail stepped into the pilothouse of the tug, shutting the door, leaving Angelina seated on Ray's crate. A vibration came from the crate. Ray was waking.

# # #

His head throbbing in pain, Ray attempted to touch it, but his hand hit something in the way. He opened his eyes to darkness, a black cloth over his head. He was on his back. His head pounded, his mouth like cotton, stomach clenched, and his broken ankle a dull pain. He held his hand in front of him, but he could only bend his forearms before touching an apparent wood wall in front of him. Feeling around with his hands and legs, he quickly realized his dilemma.

From pistol-whipped in the car to now caged in a box. His body felt heavy, the darkness was crushing all his senses. Was this his final destination? Would they bury him in this box? The air was somewhat fresh, not stuffy, but without water or food, he wouldn't last long. He breathed hard, smashing his fists against the sides of the crate, then screamed. His body trembled out of control. He rolled side to side. He heard a voice and screamed again, "Help, let me out of here."

Someone slapped the crate hard, softly said, "Quiet. You must be quiet."

A woman. He recognized Vladislav's girlfriend's voice despite being surrounded by wood on all six sides.

"Angelina, you must get me out of here. I, I, I can't stay in here." Continuing to breathe rapidly, his world began to spin.

# # #

Angelina leaned down close to the top of the box, and whispered, "You must be quiet. You will soon be aboard *Arisha*. I won't let them keep you in here, I promise, but you must be quiet."

"Who are you talking to?" Vladislav shouted from the door of the pilot house.

She glanced up at him while still seated on the crate. "Mr. Holland is awake."

"What did you say to him?"

"I told him to be quiet."

"Oh, good. Keep him that way. We can't head to *Arisha* until it gets dark."

Angelina stood. "I need to use the bathroom. May I go in the house?"

Vladislav opened the door into the pilot house and asked Mikail, then turned back. "He says first door to the right, down the hall. You are not to speak to the girls." Angelina nodded, stepped off the tug onto the dock, and walked to the house. The two young ladies were seated on a long leather couch watching an animated cartoon movie on a large TV. Cellophane baggies lay on a glass coffee table in front of them, some pills scattered loose. They stood as she stepped inside, both said, "Hi," and waved their small hands slightly.

"Hi. Bathroom?" Angelina asked. Both pointed at the hallway while seeming to scrutinize their visitor. When Angelina came out and down the hall, they stood blocking her path dressed in bikini tops, tiny shorts, hair tied back in pig tails. Angelina gazed out the slider toward the tug on the dock. Vladislav and Mikail were not in sight.

"I'm not supposed to speak to you. May I get by?"

"We won't tell," said the slightly taller girl with brown hair in pigtails with pink bows. "What is your name?"

"I'm Angelina."

"My name is Katie, and this is Natalie. Are you Mikail's new girlfriend, or are you here to work?"

Their eyes were bloodshot and glazed over. Angelina said, "I'm not either one."

"Why are you here then?" Katie asked.

Angelina stood rigid and speechless.

"Are you the special guest, cuz we're not ready for you," Natalie asked.

"No, I'm not –"

"Is the man on the boat you came with, is he...?" Natalie interrupted.

"No, we have different business with Mikail." Angelina leaned to one side, peering around the girls to check the dock, then asked, "How old are you two?"

"We're both eighteen," Katie said.

"No, I don't think so. Much younger. Now please let me by, or they will come looking for me and find me talking to you."

They stepped aside. Angelina briskly walked to the sliding door and then turned to the girls. "You two should go back to your homes." Frowning, she stepped out the glass door, and closed it.

13

The stern halogen lights of the *Arisha* glowed bright against the dark sky. The ship now faced north as the tide began to come in. The tidal change further delayed their ability to tie up and unload the crates containing the GG devices, stones, and Ray Holland.

Ray had remained silent for the entire voyage after the incident at the dock. Angelina was concerned that he lay unconscious again. She could understand how a person could panic in such a small space with no apparent escape. *I hope that never happens to me.*

After being tied to the stern line, the tug rested gently against the hull of the *Arisha*. Vladislav stepped easily onto the gangway from the bow of the tug after his crew lowered it. Angelina asked to stay on board and help load the crates onto the hoist from the stern crane. Mikail told her he appreciated the help but he could handle it by himself. When the cable came down, he grabbed it, signaling on the radio to stop.

Angelina pointed to the crate containing Ray and said, "This one should go first." Mikail shrugged, stepped around the other crates, and fastened the hook to the lines on the crate. Angelina watched closely as it rose in the shadow of the ship's hull gradually into the bright lights above. Once the crew swung it around over the ship and it was no longer over the sea, she blew a sigh of relief.

As the cable came down again, she said, "What you are doing with those girls is wrong."

"What do you know of those girls? Did they speak to you?"

"They didn't need to. I know what they are."

"They are my guests and are no concern to you. I saved them from the street, so they are happy."
Mikail waved to stop the hook as it lay slack in the tug.

"You are like Vlad's brother, different but still evil. I should save those girls."

"They don't need saving. They work, make money, I bring them friends to hang with, they are happy. So don't meddle."

Mikail pressed a button on the radio, called to lift the large crate, and it swayed between them. Once it cleared the deck Mikail grabbed Angelina by her life vest and pulled her in close. She gasped and tried to push away with both her arms.

His face held an expression of menace. "Like I said before, speak nothing of the girls, you and Vlad."

Angelina threw her right arm back, clenched a fist and swung. Mikail blocked it with his left hand, twisting it, and forced her to turn around. With his right arm, he reached around her narrow waist and pulled her in close again.

"Don't think I do not know how to handle a woman like you." She tried to pull his arm away, but he only squeezed harder. She wheezed as she tried hard to breathe. As the cable came down for the last crate, he released her.

She turned away, grumbling.

"Remember what I said."

"I will not speak of this," she agreed, then ran to the bow of the tug, and onto the gangway.

Mikail honked a loud horn from the pilot house of the tug, and *Arisha*'s crew released the line. She slowly drifted back in the darkness, only lit by her running lights against the darkness.

Angelina watched as he pulled away and spat her rage into the sea.

Vladislav waited at the top of the gangway when she stepped onto the deck. "That went well, I hope," he said.

She shrugged. "How is Mr. Holland?"

"He is breathing, I can tell. He will soon be out of the crate and into the second hold for now. We must wait as Mikail will be bringing his wife, hopefully soon."

Angelina glared at Vladislav, her lips tight.

"What is wrong?"

"You must know of those girls, what they are."

"I know, but it is not our concern. He has his business in America, we have ours. Now don't speak of this again."

Angelina scowled and then turned and walked away.

14

The gravel crunched under the tires as Chuck and Natalie drove up the long driveway to the two-story craftsman style home near Sky Londa. After Tessa explained how she blamed Ray for his carelessness, she insisted they come and check Ray's well-being, acknowledging that he might be feeling overwhelmed with guilt. Seeing the Holland's remaining functioning car, a 2004 green Subaru in the driveway, was a good sign Ray was likely home, although they understood it unlikely he was capable of driving with his cast foot. As they pulled up behind the Subaru, Chuck noticed the broken garage door.

"Stay in the car." He peered at Natalie.

"Oh my God, is Ray hurt?" Natalie covered her mouth. "Should we call 911?"

"Just hold on, I'll take a look."

Chuck peeked inside the broken door, tapped a couple times on the door frame. "Hello, Ray, it's Chuck."

The shop area was messier than he last recalled. He frowned. Ray was much more organized than to leave his shop in disorder, let alone the door broken, hanging on its brass hinges. He walked out, shrugged his shoulders toward Natalie, and waved for her to get out of the car and follow. They approached the back kitchen entry door and knocked. Greeted by an eerie silence, Chuck checked the brass doorknob. The door pushed open. He called, "Ray, anybody home?"

Again silence, so they stepped cautiously into the kitchen, then into the family room. In the study, desk drawers gaped open.

"This isn't right." Natalie put her hand to her forehead, turned, and glancd at the way they came.

Chuck nodded. "I don't think Ray would leave the house like this, even with a broken ankle. We should look upstairs."

Carefully, he led the way up the creaky steps. The door to the main bedroom was wide open, clothing scattered on the floor. Some drawers hung open on a high oak dresser, clearly containing women's garments. Natalie stepped into the bathroom and gasped. "Chuck, we need to call the police."

He stepped in behind her. Cupboards stood open, a scattering of bottles, boxes of perfume, cologne, makeup were strewn about.

"Ray wouldn't have done this, even if he was upset. This looks like a burglary, but where's Ray?"

Chuck immediately called the police, then Tessa a few minutes later. He and Natalie waited in the living room, wondering what took place.

Hearing a car approach on the driveway, they stepped out onto the covered front porch to greet a black and white Palo Alto Police cruiser. A lone officer in a dark uniform stepped out, a clipboard in his hand, and "Johnson" in white letters on his chest.

"Are you the Hollands?" the officer asked, already writing on his pad.

Natalie spoke up. "No, we're the ones who called. I'm Natalie Holmes, this is my husband Chuck. We're Tessa Holland's parents."

"Is Mrs. Holland here?"

"No," Natalie replied. "We told that to the operator. She's in the hospital."

Officer Johnson mumbled something.

"What was that, officer...Johnson?" Natalie asked.

"Oh, sorry. This is probably one of those burglaries where the perpetrators gather accident information from hospitals when the patients allow the information to be publicly released, usually intended for family inquiries."

Natalie pointed toward the open front door of the house. "Officer Johnson, if you would kindly pay attention for a moment, let me tell you what I think is happening here. Now I watch a lot of detective stories on TV, and this has kidnapping written all over it."

Chuck turned and gazed at his wife with a stupefied look. But before he could say a word, the officer dropped his clipboard to his side. "Maybe we should go inside, and you can show me how this is a kidnapping."

Natalie put her hand up to stop the progress of the officer as he stepped toward the door. Chuck almost bumped into him as he halted.

"Now hold on," Natalie scolded. "First things first. My son-in-law Ray is not here. We searched the house and garage. Second, the door to the garage has been kicked in, and things are strewn about. This is unusual for my son-in-law. That is their car in the driveway. Now him and his wife had some difficulty at the hospital, but he's a devoted husband, and wouldn't do anything stupid."

"Excuse me, Miss Natalie," he interrupted.

"Hold on, you call me Mrs. Holmes."

"Sorry, Mrs. Holmes. Everything you've described still looks like a residential burglary."

"Wait, there's more." She waved her hand to lead the officer inside. Chuck shrugged and followed.

"Now, we were careful not to touch anything, so you can collect fingerprints. But you see that wet towel on the floor?" She pointed to the white kitchen towel resting in a pool of water on the hardwood floor in the living room. "There's a stain on that towel. A blood stain. I bet it matches my son-in-law. Ray wasn't bleeding when he left the hospital. Bruised yes, bleeding no."

The officer sighed. "Okay, you two stay here while I look around."

The officer made his way into the kitchen, den, living and family room before proceeding up the creaky stairs. A few minutes later, he came down, writing some notes on his pad.

"I need to take some pictures. I'll be right back." He stepped onto the covered porch.

"Don't forget to look in the garage," Natalie shouted.

"Nat," Chuck turned toward his wife. "You've really outdone yourself here. What makes you think this is a kidnapping? Who would even want to kidnap Ray?"

"A lot of things. You just wait. I want to see how smart this officer is."

"Nat, really?" He paused. "Okay, if this is a kidnapping, don't you think we should speed things up? It's Ray we're talking about here."

"Okay, you're probably right. First thing, their passports are missing."

"How –?"

"Hold on," Natalie interrupted. "See the chair there?" She pointed to the chair in the middle of the floor. "Look at the floor, the scuff, the dent, the crack in the chair. That is one of the kitchen chairs. Why would it be here in the living room, and then somehow fall on the floor?"

"Your son-in-law is walking around on a broken ankle, remember?" Chuck offered.

"No. You aren't putting all the pieces together. This is what they do on TV. Each part by itself means little, but when you put it all together, it spells a bigger crime. Close your eyes and think about it."

"Nat, I'm not going to close my eyes. Just let the officer do his job."

"His job is to find Ray."

Officer Johnson stepped back into the living room from the front porch and held up the camera. "I covered the garage." He then stepped into the den, taking pictures of the open desk drawers, then clumped upstairs again.

A gentle knock came from the direction of the front door. "Hello?" called a tiny gray-haired woman in a pink full-length dress.

"Hello," responded Natalie. "Can we help you?"

"No, but I think I can help you." She gripped the door jamb and introduced herself as Anja Dietrich, the next-door neighbor.

"Chuck, help her inside. Let's put you here on the couch."

He held his arm out to guide the seemingly frail woman.

"I saw the police car, so I wanted to make sure everything is okay on account of what I saw earlier today. Who are you folks? You look like Tessa." Anja examined Natalie's face closely, squinting.

Natalie leaned closer. "We're her parents. This is Chuck, and I'm Natalie."

"I called 911 after what I saw, but nobody came." Her pale, wrinkled face wore a concerned look.

"What did you see?" Natalie asked as Officer Johnson stepped off the last stair.

"Who do we have here?" he interrupted.

Natalie stood and turned, facing Officer Johnson. "This is Anja Dietrich, a witness."

"A witness to what?" Officer Johnson casually asked.

"I saw this lady and man put Ray in a car and drive off. Ray was hunched over and hopping on one foot. The man was yelling at the lady in some foreign language. They put bags and buckets in the trunk and weren't gentle with Ray at all. I saw a gun."

"Whoa, hold on. Miss...?"

"Dietrich," Natalie offered.

"Miss Dietrich. You saw someone with a gun?"

"That's what I said. The yelling man had a gun in his hand, waving it around."

"Miss Dietrich, do you think you can describe the man and woman to me, what type of car it was?"

"Yes. I can give you the license plate number, make, model, and year too, if you like."

"Yes." He took the information. "I need to make some calls. You all stay right here. Don't touch anything, I'll be right back."

"You know what this means?" Natalie offered, watching Officer Johnson almost trip over the threshold.

"You were right as usual?" Chuck said.

"Someone has really kidnapped our son. We need to call Tessa."

55

15

Mikail pushed the metal gurney covered in blue blankets, a blue air cannister strapped to it with a wide belt. Neatly dressed in a blue jacket with reflective tape and an emblem reading RayMed Services, he carefully proceeded down the bright corridor of the emergency room entrance of Stanford Hospital. His colleagues at the consulate had provided him with a room, floor number, and hospital layout to locate Tessa Holland.

He walked briskly through the ER to avoid any questions. With an empty gurney, no one paid him much attention. There were plenty of patients already on gurneys, or walking around in gowns, and nurses and doctors scurrying between patient rooms. His co-worker Boris waited in the van idling in the covered entrance ready to back in when the time came. A low-cost radio was clipped to his pocket.

Arriving at a large elevator, he pressed the button for up. The door opened; the space was empty. *What luck!* He smiled, quickly pushed the gurney inside, and pressed for the first floor. Closing his eyes, he envisioned the route he'd memorized to her room.

Unfortunately, it required his passing the nurses' station. He'd been in hospitals before, even tried to check in at these stations, finding the nurses preoccupied with their computers and clipboards. He expected the same this time. He approached the nurses' station where only one nurse sat, focused on her computer screen and keyboard, hunting for the correct keys.

He looked away as he passed and turned the corner down the first corridor. Tessa's room should be the third on the left. He passed it by slowly, glancing inside. Someone lay in the bed, a woman by the length of her hair. She appeared asleep; no guests were seated in the room – a good sign. Backing up, he pushed the gurney into the room, closing the door after he entered.

Pulling out the flask with chloroform inside, he poured some on a handkerchief, stepped to the bed, and pressed it over her mouth and nose. She woke, her eyes wide, but after breathing in two strong breaths she was too weak to fight. She relaxed and went limp. As she took additional breaths, he glanced at the IV bottle hanging nearby, the heart monitor on her finger. Reaching up, he powered off the computer screen monitoring her vitals, and disconnected the IV bag, but left the catheter in her arm.

Quickly positioning the gurney next to the bed, he stripped off the sheets, rolled her onto the gurney, then wrapped her in a loose sheet. Taking the oxygen mask from the canister, he strapped it on her face, and tucked her hair neatly behind her head. It was time to go. Stepping to the door and opening it, he glanced out to more activity than he wanted to see, but he couldn't chance a wait. Sweat poured off his forehead as his anxiety kicked up.

Pushing the gurney out the door, he turned quickly, heading down the corridor, past the nurses' station to the waiting elevator. The nurse at the station glanced up at him and smiled. He nodded, smiled, stood erect, and waited in front of the elevator doors. Wiping the sweat from his forehead, he could feel his heart pounding hard.

The door opened, and he waited as a young couple in street clothes stepped off, then he pushed forward, pressing the main floor button. When the door sealed closed, he breathed a quick sigh. Pulling the two-way radio out of his jacket pocket, he called Boris to back the ambulance into position, he was on his way.

When the door opened, two security guards stood a mere ten feet away talking to a man and woman in street clothes at the check-in counter. They gave him a glance but continued talking, one guard writing on a small pad. He slipped by behind them, pushing briskly toward the ER doors, which opened automatically for him. The ambulance doors were open, the engine running, and he pushed the gurney expecting it to collapse and slide in, but it crashed hard.

#

Two floors above him the floor nurse yelled as the two security guards dressed in black uniforms exited the elevator on the third floor.

"Room 302, a man dressed at a paramedic took our patient, ten minutes ago," the older of the two guards called on the radio. "We have a patient taken by a paramedic on the third floor. Secure the hospital immediately." The security guard ordered the younger man to stay and get the patient information, and a more accurate description of the paramedic as he ran to the elevator.

A page sounded over the speakers in the ER drive: "Code Alpha, third floor, repeat code Alpha, all personnel." Mikail watched a couple of hospital staff run toward the automatic doors from the ER driveway. A paramedic team of two men stood, appearing perplexed by what was meant by the code. They ran toward the door and inside, leaving the drive empty.

Mikail ran around to the driver's door. "Help me," he called out to Boris. His cohort shifted the ambulance back into park and stepped out, running back to help.

"I can't get it to collapse."

Boris snorted. "You fool, you must lower it first."

"Show me, hurry."

Both looked underneath, trying to find the controls to lower the gurney. As they pushed levers, shaking the gurney, it suddenly dropped. They leaped back as it crashed to the concrete driveway. The carefully wrapped body bounced hard and landed face down on the concrete.

"Boris," Mikail yelled. "Look what you've done! Help me pick her up."

As Boris grasped the blanket at the head, and Mikail grabbed the dangling, sock-covered feet, a yell came from the ER entrance. Two security guards in dark uniforms and two firemen came running out.

"Stop, right now," one of the guards yelled. The firemen in full gear were about to overtake the slower-running guards.

"Boris, time to go, leave her."

Boris dropped the body to the concrete, raced around to the open driver's door and jumped in, shifting the ambulance into drive. Mikail opened the passenger door and with one foot on the threshold, Boris accelerated. Mikail held hard to the door, almost falling off the now-speeding ambulance.

"Slow down, you fool, let me get in," Mikail yelled.

As Boris braked hard, the door flew forward. Mikail held the door as it protested in a loud groan from his weight. Mikail twisted his body to watch as the guards and firemen attended to his kidnap victim. He slid into the seat and grunted as he tried to shut the door. It wouldn't close. He sighed.

\# \# \#

The firemen and guards carefully assessed the woman who remained face down. A triage nurse came running out, and helped gently roll her over onto a backboard. Her nose was scraped and bleeding.

"Who is she?" one of the firemen asked. "Why would they try to take her?"

"It's Ms. Rollins. Ma'am, can you hear me?" the nurse asked. There was no response. "We need to get her inside right away."

16

The crunch of gravel broke the quiet of the rural neighborhood, the pink sky beginning to darken. The yellow cab driver spoke, "Hey lady, we're here."

Tessa raised her head from the daze brought on by exhaustion and the pain meds for her bone-bruised left arm.

What's with all these cars here at home? Then she remembered the phone call from her mother – a break-in, and Ray was missing. She still couldn't shake some of the anger, wanting to blame someone for her loss. He, however, needed to take some responsibility for what had happened. And if not, then things might be over for them. She cringed as her stomach contracted again. Maybe her body reminding her who to blame. And what if they separated? She could make it with her part-time job at Stanford and take half her million dollars from selling the road sealant formula she'd created. She didn't need Ray...or did she?

A voice called out, breaking her thought, a familiar face, her mother. Mom and Dad walked off the porch toward her.

"You can't stay here Tessa, it's too dangerous," Mom insisted as Tessa remained in the taxi with the door open.

"Dangerous?"

"Yes. Ray's been kidnapped by Russians," she blurted. "They might come back for you."

"Mom, wait. Russians, what Russians?"

"The police, thanks to your neighbor Anja, traced the rental they took Ray in, to an Angelina Nikitin, with a Moscow address."

"They told you that?"

Dad stepped forward, reaching to help Tessa out of the taxi, the driver fidgeting, clearly eager to leave.

"Um, your mother was pretty much in Officer Johnson's face, since she felt she cracked the case." He wrinkled his brow.

"Dad, could you pay the driver?" Tessa asked. "I need to go inside and see what's going on."

Natalie grabbed her arm. "No, honey, you can't go inside. They're still processing the crime scene. Fingerprints and evidence."

"How long does it take to do all this? I want to go inside. It's getting dark."

"I know. We've been sitting on the porch this whole time. Anja brought over some sweet tea, though. She's so nice. You really owe her."

"Owe her?"

Mom blocked her way. "Yes. Weren't you listening? Are you okay?"

"Sorry. They gave me some Percocet before I left the hospital. I'm a bit drowsy."

"We'll just take you to our house. We can come back in the morning," Mom offered.

Tessa agreed without argument. They started toward the Holmeses' blue Toyota Prius when Officer Johnson came running over. "Is this Mrs. Holland?"

Mom stopped him. "Yes, but she's going with us. She needs some rest."

"Hold on, we need to bring you all up to speed on the investigation."

"Can you make it fast?" Mom insisted.

"Okay. We called the FBI for some assistance on this since there's foreign involvement. Special Agent Bryce Hamilton is at Ms. Dietrich's home building a profile." He looked at his clip board and flipped a page. "He's also taken a lead role in the investigation, which we're grateful for. You'll still need to do a police report with Palo Alto regarding items stolen and contact your insurance company. We'll lock up when we're done tonight, but expect activity here tomorrow as our joint investigation may continue."

Dad thanked Officer Johnson and received his business card and one for Special Agent Hamilton. A moment later, they drove away under the darkened sky.

17

The car was quiet as Dad turned into the gravel driveway in the bright morning sun. The two-story Holland home threw long shadows across the yard. A Santa Clara sheriff's sedan sat idling in front of the garage. A tall, bleached blond-haired man opened the car door and stepped out to greet the unknown visitors.

Taking in the scene from the back seat, Tessa wept. Her mother turned and patted her leg. Dad stopped the car just before blocking the sheriff's vehicle, and he got out to talk to the deputy.

"What's wrong, honey?" Her mother held out a tissue.

"Mom. Is this all just a bad dream? I feel I've lost everything in the course of a few days. My husband, my baby, our home is the center of an investigation...my baby..." Tessa continued to weep. "This is my fault, my fault."

"This is not your fault, Tess. This is just...bad people doing evil things."

"Me. I'm the evil one here." Her chin trembled.

"Heaven forbid. You're not the evil one...stop with that."

"Mom, you don't understand. I blamed Ray for our baby's death...I told him to leave...more than once. He was in a wheelchair. He was hurting too. How insensitive of me. If he had stayed at the hospital, he would have found out the baby didn't die from the accident. There was a developmental issue. The baby would have aborted on its own. He'd still be here." Covering her face, she continued to sob.

"Tessa. Honey, we're going to get through this." Mom glanced out the window at the deputy's hand motions while he spoke with Dad in front of the car. Dad glanced toward the car and pointed to the house. She turned toward Tessa.

"Okay, honey, it looks like we can go inside. Let's go get some clothes and makeup. Whatever you need, then we'll go get breakfast."

Without a word, Tessa opened the door and stepped into the growing brightness of the sun. Dad greeted them. "So, we can go inside and get what we need but be careful what we touch. If we find anything unusual, we're to let him know. He said the FBI will be here soon to wrap up the site."

Stepping inside the front door, Tessa shivered at the thought of the intrusion. She stared at the items out of place - the broken chair in the living room, drawers open in Ray's office. She rushed up the narrow stairway to their bedroom, stopping at the doorway, and covered her mouth. Drawers open, clothes scattered. The bathroom counters a mess of perfume bottles toppled, cleansers, hair color, and lipstick. Stepping over strewn clothes and underwear on the floor, she entered the walk-in closet and drew a large breath.

"Why would they take my clothes and cosmetics?" she asked Mom who had arrived at the doorway, catching her breath.

A wooden jewelry box lay open on top of the dresser, red felt lined drawers open, some pulled completely out, and contents strewn on the floor.

"Now this makes more sense," Tessa said. "A burglary. Go for the jewelry box, clothes, perfume. Who are these people?"

Her mother touched Tessa's arm. "Honey, we'll help you get this all put back together as soon as we can. All this can be replaced."

"Ray. What about Ray, Mom? He might be dead on my account."

A voice from downstairs yelled, "FBI is here."

Mom led her down the stairwell, with Tessa's right hand on her shoulder, to the living room. Dad was shaking hands with a lean dark-haired man in a blue suit jacket, shiny black shoes, and beige khakis.

Reaching out his hand, he approached Tessa and her mother. "You must be Natalie Holmes, and Tessa Holland, Ray's wife?"

Tessa glanced at her mother, noticing her infatuation as Mom smiled at the young agent with a tanned complexion, large hands and well-developed arms. Despite her chaotic thoughts, Tessa couldn't ignore the attraction.

"I'm FBI special Agent Bryce Hamilton. We've taken a lead in the investigation. As it appears, we have a federal crime here involving foreigners."

Tessa spoke up. "When can I have my home back?"

"We're all done here, or at least I'm all done. I'm the sole agent on this case, working out of the Palo Alto field office."

"You seem awfully young to be working alone." Mom turned her bright smile on him.

"I graduated from the Academy last year, near the top of the class. Only moved here a month ago. I think I made some of the older agents uncomfortable, or at least that's my take on the move. It's okay by me. I like the quiet time to review case notes carefully."

"What do you know about my husband?" Tessa asked, ready for some good news.

"Not too much yet. A rental car was dropped off at the Bais Marina, ordered by a native Russian Angelina Nikitin. Probably came in by ship. San Francisco's main port office is running through manifests looking for ships matching the arrival period. I'm afraid the list will be long, as the port is busy. Also, customs are struggling to find the I-94 she would have filled in upon arrival."

"Any idea why they took Ray?" Tessa asked.

"I have information stating you were kidnapped a year ago by a Russian, Viktor Mishkin, then rescued by your husband. Viktor was killed by blunt force trauma that couldn't be explained.

Apparently caused by some device of your husband's. I'm wondering if this is linked somehow. They were seen loading some items from your garage."

"Oh no." Tessa gulped.

"What?" Agent Hamilton asked.

"Everything in the garage involves Ray's project."

"This project, the same that this Viktor stole last year?"

"No. Viktor Mishkin destroyed that project. Ray is still developing a new prototype, but he's nowhere close to what he had before."

"Is this project dangerous?"

Tessa tried to see a connection, but the ongoing questions and her hunger kept breaking her concentration. Glancing up blankly at the agent, she didn't answer.

"Okay then, we'll come back to that."

"Actually, your predecessors last year collected information regarding Ray's project. I'm sure there's a file somewhere you can read and make those types of determinations," Tessa offered.

Her mother raised her hand. "Aren't you going to go to the marina, since that's where the rental originated from?"

"I will, but without physical resources, the Bay Area is too large to cover alone. If I get the name of a ship, then I'll call in the Coast Guard and ask the port authority to hold the ship."

Mom stepped forward. "We can help."

Dad placed his hand on Mom's shoulder from behind, which she pushed away with a stern glance.

"I'm afraid your direct involvement wouldn't be safe." Hamilton maintained a stoic expression.

Mom frowned. "Why not just hold all the Russian ships?"

"I wish it was that easy. We don't know what ship or registration they came in on."

Weakness washed over Tessa, and she glanced at the couch. "Mom, I need to either sit or go get breakfast before I fall down."

Dad stepped forward. "Let's lock up, go get breakfast, then come back for the items you need to stay at the house."

Hamilton agreed and reassured them that the sheriff's deputy would stay to watch the place for the time being. Mom let out a noticeable sigh, then gently led Tessa to their car.

# # #

Hamilton sat in his car reviewing his notes before heading to the port customs office to check on updates when his cell phone rang. It was a Sergeant Gunderson from the Palo Alto Police Department calling from Stanford Hospital about a kidnapping attempt involving a patient. Hamilton assured him he would arrive at the scene shortly.

18

Agent Hamilton pulled into a parking stall outside the emergency room entrance labeled "Doctor Parking Only." Having a California license registration on his car, he wasn't concerned about it being towed. He noticed several Palo Alto police cruisers in the same parking lot, a few officers milling about the sliding door entrance. Approaching the two uniformed Palo Alto officers he asked, "Sergeant Gunderson?"

"Inside." One of the officers pointed toward the sliding doors.

Scanning the arrival area, he saw an officer speaking with a hospital staff member dressed in blue scrubs and white tennis shoes. Another officer with three chevrons on his uniform stood nearby. *This must be Gunderson.* Stepping toward them, he pulled out his FBI credentials and displayed them once the man glanced in his direction.

"Agent Hamilton?" He stepped forward. "Thanks for coming so quickly."

"I was in the area." He made eye contact with the hospital staffer.

"Oh, this is Nurse Hernandez. She treated a Ms. Rollins, the patient these men tried to kidnap."

"Are you done with your interviews so we can sit down and review this?" Hamilton asked.

"Yes. Let's go sit down." He pointed toward a door labeled "Private."

The space appeared more like a patient's room than something to use for information gathering, but being out of the public eye and having some privacy to discuss a criminal investigation suited him fine.

"So, what do you have?" Hamilton asked as they sat down at a small white table.

"Not much. A Ms. Rollins, a patient on the third floor recovering from appendicitis.
Single, unmarried, no children, Interior decorator, self-employed."

Hamilton made a note on his note pad. "The kidnappers?"

"An ambulance driver and paramedic in a RayMed Services Ambulance. No plate info, but we did find out RayMed had a similar ambulance stolen three years ago from their San Francisco office. It was never recovered."

Gunderson pulled a pen from his shirt pocket, scribbled indecipherably on his notes, and flipped the page. "A BOLO on the vehicle has turned up nothing so far. The driver, Caucasian, short light hair, dark blue uniform, black and white tennis shoes. The paramedic was the one who arrived on the third floor with a gurney; nobody questioned his reason for being there. Just one nurse at the nurse's station saw him leave with Ms. Rollins on the gurney."

Hamilton stopped writing, reached up and rubbed his chin. "Seems the Hospital needs to review security procedures."

"Apparently, there was a code blue, unresponsive, on the floor fifteen minutes earlier, which explained the shortness of staff at the time, maybe a reason for a slip up. The guy had balls though. How would he know of a distraction, unless he created it." Gunderson made another note.

Hamilton motioned his hand in a circle. "Go on…"

"He was Caucasian, short blond hair. Plain features, taller, maybe five-feet-ten, wearing a blue jacket with the ambulance service emblem. The nurse is working with our illustrator to put together a composite, but she's sure she's never seen him before."

"So, what went wrong with the kidnapping since Ms. Rollins is still here?"

"When the fake paramedic arrived at the ambulance, he and the other man appeared to be having issues with collapsing the gurney. About the same time, the staff discovered Ms. Rollins missing and alerted the entire hospital. Fortunately, the men were spotted in the Emergency Room driveway, and they panicked when approached. Ms. Rollins fell off the gurney and sustained minor injuries, but she'll be okay. The oddest thing about all of this is Ms. Rollins was just put in that room after coming out of surgery. She hadn't been in there an hour."

"So, she could have been selected by mistake then?" Hamilton asked.

"Appears possible."

"Like I said before, the hospital should review their security policies, everyone's movements, and spot check staff identifications. Have you looked into the patient list on this floor for what you think would be a more likely value target for a kidnap attempt?"

"We did. Most of this floor's patients are coming out of surgery or the ER, so not in the best shape to go anywhere."

"Who was in that room prior to Ms. Rollins?"

Gunderson flipped a page on his tablet and read, "A Tessa Holland."

Hamilton' face went cold; he stared at Sergeant Gunderson. "Are you sure?"

"Says right here, checked out at 10:45 by a Dr. Gabriela, and the floor nurse's name is on the release as well. Are you thinking they were here to take Holland?"

"Yes. I have to go." Hamilton rose and raced to the elevator.

19

Hamilton hurried to his Ford, which was still parked in the doctor slip near the entrance of the ER. He had just finished his phone call with the Santa Clara sheriff's deputy who was staked out at the Holland house. Hamilton had informed him about the attempted kidnapping of Mrs. Holland at Stanford Hospital. The deputy mentioned there had been no activity at the home, and Mrs. Holland had not returned with her parents.

Recalling they planned to get food, there was no telling where they were, but he felt the kidnappers wouldn't know either. He looked up and dialed Tessa's phone number. After three rings it went to a voice mail message recorded in a man's voice, likely Ray's. Slamming his fist against the steering wheel, he scanned his notes. There were no other numbers for Tessa Holland. He did have a number for Natalie Holmes. He dialed.

"Hello," the voice answered.

"Natalie Holmes, this is Special Agent Hamilton."

"Oh hello, Agent Hamilton." Her voice took on a cheery note.

"Where are you?" he asked.

"Oh, we're here at Dinah's over on El Camino Real. They have a pool here, you know."

"Is Tessa with you?" he asked.

"Of course. She's feeling much better now after finishing off her pancake order and espresso. You know she wanted a burger, but I insisted on breakfast. I can't stand the smell of burnt beef this early."

"Stay there until I get there," he commanded.

"Sure. Can I order something for when you arrive?"

"That won't be necessary. Just stay there." Hamilton hung up and sped out of the parking lot.

He drove once around Dinah's Garden Hotel, scanning the parking lot for an ambulance, although he was confident it wouldn't be there. He had to verify. Already he sensed he was falling behind in the investigation of the Holland kidnapping. He needed Tessa safe.

Seeing the white umbrellas over tables around the pool and garden area, he bypassed checking in with the restaurant hostess and stepped onto a concrete path leading to the pool area. The pool lay quiet as no guests were swimming this early, and not a soul lay stretched out on any of the white lounge chairs. Several tables were occupied by guests eating and drinking, and surprisingly, there were no young children running about. It was then he heard a shout.

"Over here, Agent," Natalie called.

As he approached, he noticed all the plates gone, only drinks in front of the three of them. Chuck Holmes had a ceramic cup of coffee, Natalie and Tessa with tall clear glasses of orange-colored drinks with ice.

"Glad you could make it." Natalie lifted her glass toward the agent. "Are you sure we can't we order you something – a Mimosa?"

"No, thanks." He pulled out one of the blue bamboo chairs and sat. He looked at Tessa. "I need your cell phone number."

Tessa lifted her glass. "Why, of course."

Natalie pointed toward Tessa's glass, held up two fingers so Hamilton could see.

"It was the only way we could get her to quit crying," she offered.

He rubbed the back of his neck. "I'm afraid there's been an incident likely related to Ray's kidnapping."

Chuck furrowed his brow while the two ladies' reaction was slowed by the alcohol; their eyes opened wider. Hamilton went on to explain the attempted kidnapping at Stanford Hospital as they all listened carefully.

"I've come to the realization they knew you were at the hospital, maybe even what floor and room, information probably provided by Ray. What they didn't know was what you look like, otherwise when they grabbed Ms. Rollins, they would have discovered the mistake. Neither of these two men matched the description of the man who took Ray. So, we need to proceed carefully with four suspects now to be on the lookout for. And Tessa, we need eyes on you at all times, so I recommend you stay away from your Sky Londa home for now. I wouldn't even recommend staying with your parents."

"Where is she to go then?" Natalie asked.

"I recommend a hotel, registered under a different name."

"We could stay with her. How about here? This is a nice place," Natalie offered.

"I wouldn't recommend that. The kidnappers may use you to find Mrs. Holland."

"Call me Tessa. Mrs. Holland sounds like I'm your teacher," Tessa interrupted.

Natalie reached out and touched Tessa's hand. "You are a teacher, remember."

"Mom, I'm the mother of a dead baby, soon to be a widow, and soon to be a victim of bad guy Russians." She slammed her glass down, spilling some of the Mimosa onto the table.

Hamilton reached over, placed his big hand on Tessa's free hand, and squeezed it. "No one is going to hurt you, I promise."

Tessa gazed into his eyes, held the stare, then placed her cold wet drink hand on his, dropped her face onto them, and sobbed. Natalie stood, walked around behind Tessa, and rubbed her back. "You heard the man, Tessa, everything is going to be okay."

Tessa lifted her head slightly. "Who's going to save Ray, while he's protecting me. Who?"

"That's a good question," Agent Hamilton said. "I'm going to the office to file my reports. It's likely the FBI will place additional resources on these cases. In the meantime, let's get Tessa checked in here as Mrs. Hamilton while I work on a different ID.

They all stood, Tessa a little unsteady. "I need to go lie down I think."

Hamilton spoke to the desk manager at the Dinah's Garden Hotel host counter while Chuck and Natalie escorted Tessa to her room. After pocketing a second key to the room, he followed a short distance behind, paying attention to the hotel layout and relevance to Tessa's room. As he stepped into the room, Tessa was already collapsed on the queen-size bed, her eyes closed. He told Chuck and Natalie not to stay or return to the hotel unless absolutely necessary. They all quietly stepped out of the room. Hamilton checked the door to be sure it locked, then his phone rang.

He answered. "Yes sir, right away."

20

Hamilton reviewed his notes, drinking coffee while waiting anxiously for this meeting to end before it had begun. He could only think of Tessa alone at the hotel while the kidnappers were loose in the city. Special Agent Steve Anderson ordered all available agents to this meeting, and finally he walked in.

"Morning everyone," Anderson called, halting the soft chatter of the agents. "We've had some exciting news this week with a sighting of Mr. Diego Guzman, wanted for the murder of Special Agent Vincent Ricci in May last year. He was spotted on the street in the financial district by local police on Wednesday afternoon, then again Friday in front of Benny's Bar at the wharf. Everything we have on him is in your packet. Whatever you have going, set it aside. You are all assigned to this case this week."

Hamilton raised his hand. "Agent Anderson, I have a US citizen kidnapping by a Russian pair, as well as a second kidnapping attempt in the span of two days. Wouldn't this take priority over this manhunt?"

"No," Anderson quickly responded. "I know all about your case, more than you realize. Currently, there's not enough information to assign resources to it. What we do have is a drug cartel member and murderer of one of our own agents in our city. I am assigning all resources to this."

If he really knew all the circumstances of my case, he would let me go. Not sit here and waste valuable time. "Sir, Mrs. Holland has lost her husband, baby, and father-in-law all in the course of a couple of days. An attempt to kidnap her was made as well. Don't we, as the FBI, have any compassion for U.S citizens affected by foreigners on our soil?"

"Agent Hamilton, I understand you're new to the Bureau, and each case you get in your small office in Palo Alto warrants priority, but not now, and not when I'm in charge of this district. Now get on board."

Hamilton's jaw tightened, his hands clenched into tight fists, not liking the authority being pushed around in front of him. He had hoped he could work from his Palo Alto office, then he could continue working on the Holland cases while handling these other assigned duties. He frowned and slumped into his chair.

Much to his relief, Anderson took the five local agents and assigned them stakeout duties on a revolving schedule. He was to work the phones, gathering intelligence from either the San Francisco office or Palo Alto. He chose Palo Alto. Anderson dismissed the group but asked him to stay for a moment. Standing, he waited as the others made their way to the door. Anderson shook a few hands, then stepped to the door, closing it.

He approached, rotating his right shoulder until it produced a cracking noise, then remained motionless, wearing a pained expression.

"Agent Hamilton. Don't take these cases that come into your office so personally. You need to focus on the greater good when it comes to the Bureau. Remember, I report directly to Director Manchester. You don't want me mentioning your name in vain in any reports presented to his office."

Hamilton clenched his fists briefly and glanced past the agent toward the door.

"I've met Mr. and Mrs. Holland. I know of the Russian involvement surrounding them and Holland's work with the government contractor. Trust me, we have feelings at the Bureau, but I need you on this case."

Hamilton looked to the door again, ready to reach for the handle. Anderson stepped into his view, held up his hand.

"We capture or kill Guzman, you can return to this case full time. In the meantime, work the phones and tip lines. If we receive verifiable information concerning the Holland case, let's evaluate it for relevance. And if by chance the Holland case has moved offshore, we contact the US State Department for assistance. But you need to keep the Guzman case a priority. Do you understand?"

"Yes, sir." His stomach tightened as he thought of Tessa alone at the hotel. He needed to find a balance between the assignments, but protecting Tessa was a priority.

21

Agent Hamilton slammed the phone down and glared out the window of his Palo Alto field office at a light rain shower passing through. Out of the twenty-three tip calls they'd received about Diego Guzman, only two seemed genuine. The remainder were simply concerned callers reporting an unfamiliar Hispanic man in their neighborhood. No tips had come in on the Holland case. He needed to make calls back to the San Francisco Port authority on the possible ship the two Russians may have taken Ray Holland to. About to pick up the desk phone, his cell rang in his pocket.

"Special Agent Hamilton," he answered.

"Agent Hamilton, Sergeant Gunderson, glad I caught you. It looks like we caught a break on the kidnap attempt at Stanford Hospital. We found several old prints on the gurney, but two more recent – one partial, and one full."

Hamilton sat bolt upright. "Yes?"

"We received a hit on the full print to a man named Boris Smirnov, a Russian national who works at the consulate in San Francisco. The prints came from a three-year-old San Francisco police file on a suspected murder charge. Nothing ever came of it, and the charges were dropped, but they processed his prints. We called the consulate, but they haven't been very helpful. They wouldn't even confirm he is in the country."

At last, the break he needed.

"Does the police file have his picture?"

"It does. I can send it to your email."

"Yes, please. Bolo?" His heart raced at the thought of a needed sighting.

"Already on it. Maybe we can catch another break and pick him up for questioning. From the physical description on file and based on witness statements, it looks like he was the driver."

He tapped his pen on the desktop. "But nothing on the other guy, other than a possible Russian connection?"

"Not so far. Might be the other print, but it's a partial and going to take longer if we get anything to match."

"Thanks for your help. Let me know if anything else comes up."

"I will."

Hamilton ended the call. Consulate involvement only meant one thing: CIA. He glanced at his computer and noticed the messages were still piling in, most of which were from the Guzman hot line. Not wanting to waste more time listening and following up on every call, he punched in the CIA's number.

On a hunch, he provided them with the old Holland case file, dropping the name Victor Mishkin as a possible link to the Holland kidnapping. They promised they would let him know.

After ending the call, he returned to listening to the Guzman calls, taking notes, and making more calls. The only satisfaction he felt was the CIA now had a name of a Russian National to track down.

Deciding to knock out just a half dozen more calls, he would drive to the hotel and check on Tessa.

22

Hamilton tapped at the door, pressed the card key into the door slot, and pushed it open. The sheets on the queen size bed were rumpled, but no Tessa. The bathroom door was shut, so he stepped close, tapped, and called out, "Tessa?" He waited, called again. He tried the doorknob. It turned, and he pushed it open. His eyes widened.

She sat in the bathtub, her knees held close to her chest. The tub held a few inches of water, and her blue jeans and light blue blouse were soaked. Her long, dark, straight hair lay wet over her knees, and her body shivered. As he kneeled beside her, she glanced up. He flipped a chrome lever to release the water. Reaching up, he grasped one of the white heavy towels from a metal rack and wrapped it around her shoulders.

"What are you doing?" He felt a fire inside him as he realized he should have been there for her sooner.

"I don't remember," she stuttered, gazing at him through bloodshot eyes.

"We need to get you out of these wet clothes and warm you up. Can you undress yourself?"

"I can't move my fingers." Her hands were clenched tightly.

"Are you okay with me helping you?"

"Please."

Hamilton placed his arm under her legs, reached around her back and lifted her easily. He rotated his body and leaned over to lower her legs to the floor. Once he felt her weight shift to her feet, he pulled her to a stand. Stepping in front, he unbuttoned her blouse and drew it off her shoulders. It crumpled to the linoleum floor. He glanced away from an obvious stare at her wet, thin bra and turned his attention to her skinny blue jeans.

After unbuttoning and unzipping the jeans, he pointed to the toilet for her to sit, which she slowly did. Carefully he worked them off, shimmying them from the hips to her knees to her ankles. Her bare legs reflected white from the chill and the bright bathroom lights. Lifting her off the toilet, he turned her around and began to pull off her pink panties.

She placed her cold hand on his. "Stop, I think it better that I take these off in private."

"Sorry, you need to get your body warmed up."

Grabbing the other towel, he dried her long straight dark hair, then rubbed her body to increase circulation. As an afterthought, he reached over and turned on the heat lamp. With the towel barely covering her nakedness, she turned around, and hugged him tight as both towels fell to the floor. He slowly encircled her shoulders and pulled her in close. She remained in damp underwear in his embrace for a couple minutes. His thin jacket was drenched.

She looked up at him and smiled. "Sorry about all this."

"It's all right. All in the line of duty."

"Is it?" She continued to gaze into his eyes.

"It...is." He released his grip, bent to pick up one of the towels, and wrapped it around her chest and waist.

Tessa let out a snorted laugh. "This is so humiliating. You know what would be funny right now?

"What?"

"If my parents showed up."

"That would require some explaining. You don't have a change of clothes, do you?"

"That was our plan until you made me stay here."

"Sorry. Let me take your clothes down to the desk and get them laundered. I'll be back in a few minutes."

"Hang on." She gently pushed him out of the bathroom, only closing the door partially. She tossed her bra and panties out the door, then stepped out and sat on the edge of the bed, wrapped in one of the towels. He placed her clothes in a courtesy plastic bag provided by the hotel and left.

23

Ray opened his eyes, surrounded in blackness, his head pulsing in pain. His chest was wrapped in oily-smelling heavy rope. It hurt to breathe. His nostrils filled with a combination of dampness, mustiness, a hint of sea air, and the scent of diesel fuel. *What is this place?* He remembered the short ride to the end of his driveway, Vladislav arranging a kidnapping of Tessa, his outburst, then darkness.

A resounding boom reverberated. He jerked. *What was that?* He listened as the noises changed, now a deep rumble followed by a continuous clunk, clunk, clunk. A long, low-frequency ship's horn blared. The chamber now vibrated steadily. *I must be aboard the vessel Vladislav mentioned - the Arisha.* He reached painfully behind his back as he attempted to work at untying the ropes with his free hands.

Then he heard another loud clunk, followed by a creaking sound, as if an old prison cell door was being opened. A burst of radiant light pierced through the blackness, taking the shape of a rectangle. A lone figure stood in the light. Ray squinted and held his hand up to block the brightness. "Hello?"

"Shh," the voice said. The legs of the figure were outlined against the luminous glow of a lantern the person carried. Too thin for a man. A young woman's legs. It had to be Angelina. The co-conspirator of his kidnapping.

She placed the lantern at his feet. "How's your head?"

"It hurts. Why did Vladislav have to hit me?"

"I'm sorry. He does not tell me his plan. He had to get you on *Arisha* in secret. His method. Are you hungry?"

"Can I have some water?"

"I have water in bottle. You do not want *Arisha* water, it tastes bad. I have food for you."

Angelina lifted the fluorescent lamp to Ray's face. She softly traced her fingers from his forehead to his cheek.

"I will clean this up and get you some ice for that bump." She lowered the lantern to the floor at his feet.

"Thank you. Why are you so nice to me when you know I'm going to die?"

"Shh." She leaned in and kissed his temple. "You be good, maybe you live. I come right back."

Leaving the lantern, Angelina walked toward the open lighted doorway. Ray's chest tingled. A feeling he'd not had in some years, not since Tessa surprise-kissed him at coffee at Stanford University, their first unofficial date. He shook his head, trying to release the feeling; everything about it was wrong. He was married to Tessa, even if she hated him for causing the death of their baby.

Angelina's image appeared in the doorway again, a tray in one hand and a bottle in the other. Setting the tray on Ray's lap, she opened the bottle, and held it out for him. He took a long swig, emptying half the contents without a breath. Angelina picked up a cool, wet towel from the tray and pressed it gently against his swollen temple. He flinched. Placing her other hand behind his head, she stroked it up and down while pressing the towel gently. Chills ran down his spine. He tried to shake it off again, but more sensations spread throughout his body.

"What happens next?" he asked quickly, trying to clear his confused thoughts.

"Do not know. We must leave America quickly, Vlad said. Mikail told Vlad he was unable to take your wife from hospital. Now many police at hospital and your home. Mikail's friend at consulate said a call came looking for me, my name. Vlad fears it won't take long to find us without cargo, so we must leave. I guess your wife won't be joining us."

"Did Vlad really think he could kidnap Tessa too?"

"Oh, yes. He was eager to please his father with a young woman. But he has you and your jewels. We head to Russia now. Once safe distance from America, he will relax, so safer for me to stay away for now."

She placed the ice filled towel in Ray's hand, picked up a spoon from the tray, swirled it in a chunky broth, and brought it to his lips. Ray opened, welcoming any nourishment to satisfy his hollow stomach. Beef, potatoes, carrots, a familiar soup of his youth, tasted remarkable.

"You like?" Angelina dipped the spoon for a second scoop. Ray nodded, swallowing.

"The only thing good on *Arisha*, thanks to Dominique. He's not pleasant to my eyes, but he's 'Master of the Mess,' they say. You should taste his *Ptichye Moloko*. A fine cake. Maybe I get you some. Dominique paid dock man in Tacoma port special in American dollars for what he needed, so he could make. I think the crew like Dominique more than me. If I could only cook." She waved the empty spoon around as she spoke.

Ray gently grabbed her forearm, then the spoon to eat on his own.

Her face flushed slightly in the lantern's glow. "Sorry," she said, as Ray scooped several spoonsful. "Does your wife cook?"

"Yes."

"Would you marry her if she did not?"

Ray stopped eating, glanced at Angelina's questioning expression, contemplating.

He offered a careful, "Yes."

"Oh good." Angelina smiled.

A horn sounded, echoing in the dark space.

"Ah, American pilot must be off *Arisha* now. Captain will be pleased."

"Angelina," Ray asked. "Will I be tied up in this dungeon for the entire trip to Russia?"

"Oh, no. Once *Arisha* far from America, we move you to regular quarters. I told Vlad he must treat you better, or no sex. He only laughed. Leonid was to watch you, but I offered him some women's clothes. Vlad does not know."

"Your clothes?"

"Oh, um, sorry. Some of your wife's." She placed her hand over her mouth and nose.

Ray rolled his eyes. "Depending on what you gave him, she may not miss them."

"Brassiere and panties."

"She'll notice." He laughed.

"At least if Vlad finds them, he knows not mine. He would kill me for sure. You will see Leonid, but he won't hurt you. He may be angry, mostly since you are here."

"Does the crew know who I am and why I'm here?"

"Probably. Secrets not well kept on *Arisha*. Vlad may offer money to keep secret."

"Angelina, you said I could live if I'm good. What do you mean?"

"Shh." She leaned in and placed her hand gently on his shoulder. "Do not say to anyone. I must go or Vlad will come. Eat, I will be back." Her slim silhouette, with shapely thighs, swayed toward the lighted doorway. Instead of closing it, she left it open, allowing light to fill the dark, echoing space. Knowing there was no place to really go, tied to a chair with a slowly healing ankle and aching chest, he continued to eat the remaining stew and sliced bread.

He pondered her mentioning the police at his home and hospital. What would they have discovered? If they knew he was on the *Arisha*, the Coast Guard would stop them soon. This nightmare would be over, or at least his imprisonment. But what of Tessa? His mourning mother? The dull rumbling of the diesel engines turned up to a louder, steadier pace. Full speed, he figured. They had cleared the channel toward the open sea. Time to Russia? Could they do 40 knots in this old rustic tub? Maybe. *Help needs to come soon.*

24

Agent Hamilton tapped on the door, opening it with the key card. Tessa was wrapped in a white towel from her chest to her thighs and seated in a soft lounge chair, her legs crossed. Hamilton smiled.

Tessa stared at him. "What's that about?"

"Nothing."

"A smile for nothing? I promise if I can go home, the next time you see me, I'll be more presentable."

"You look fine. I'm just glad you're not back in the tub."

She frowned. "I said I was sorry about all this."

"Don't worry about it. Your clothes will be done in about two hours. I can turn up the heat in here if you're cold."

"I already did. Plus, I called down to the desk for a bathrobe. They actually said they have one to bring me."

"Have your parents called?"

"No."

"Good. The less information the kidnappers can collect regarding your location the better off we are keeping you here."

A knock came at the door. Tessa sat forward to get up, and her towel partially unwrapped.

Hamilton threw up his hand to stop her. "I'll get it."

"It's probably the bathrobe." She attempted to get the towel wrapping re-adjusted.

Hamilton opened the door, and a young man in the familiar attire of the staff at Dinah's stood, holding a white bathrobe across his arm. With wide eyes, he looked past Hamilton as Tessa adjusted her towel. Hamilton turned, noticing more skin than this man should be staring at, and whipped the bathrobe off his arm. "It's not a show here."

The young man said, "Sorry," as he slammed the door shut.

"Oops, I was just trying to get this back on." She kept fiddling with the towel. He did his best to not stare.

"I'll take that." She reached for the bathrobe. In doing so, the towel slipped open, and she clutched it to her chest before it fell completely to the floor.

Hamilton turned his head.

She gave a little giggle. "It's not like you haven't already seen all this.

"Not all of it," he said, his head still turned away.

"We're Mr. And Mrs. Hamilton, right?" She laughed. "If anybody is watching."

"So far, just the hotel employee."

"I bet the staff at hotels have loads of stories. Decent now."

Hamilton turned around and smiled. "You look great in that bathrobe. I know that has to be warmer than the damp towel."

"It is." She sat back down on the soft fabric chair and crossed her legs. "Now what?"

Hamilton's phone buzzed. He pulled it out of his pocket looked at the display, then answered. "Special Agent Hamilton."

"Agent Hamilton, this is CIA Foreign Intelligence Officer Ricardo. I was given a couple names, one a Russian National, and one a Russian citizen you were seeking information regarding."

"Yes." He covered the phone with his hand and mouthed the letters "CIA" to Tessa.

"We haven't found much on Boris Smirnov other than time in the country, working at the consulate in San Francisco. What is interesting about Boris is both times he's been held for questioning by local PD – once for a murder investigation, the other for a domestic violence charge - he was picked up by a Mikail Sokolov. This Mikail Sokolov has been on our radar for a while. Possible international drug and child trafficking. Recently employed at the consulate, but we've never seen him come and go when we watched the place. It's a stretch, but he might be relevant in the kidnap attempt at Stanford Hospital."

"Excuse me, Officer Recardo," Hamilton interrupted, "But would you happen to have a picture of Mikail? I could show it around at the hospital and see if we have a match."

"I do. I'll email it you. We also just received an anonymous tip through the local PD on a location for Mikail and other information sensitive to the investigation. Now as far as Dimitri Mishkin and his son Viktor, they go way back. Viktor dead of course. Dimitri runs a shipping business from Moscow. He has another son, Vladislav, who works for him, likely on one of his ships. He has small fleet of three ships that have conducted business with the US, including a ship named *Arisha* which recently came into San Francisco Bay and anchored."

"That has to be the ship they took Ray Holland to." Hamilton stepped to the nightstand, grabbed the courtesy hotel room pen and pad, and wrote.

"I don't have the current status, but she steamed in here a couple days ago."

"Thanks, Officer Ricardo. I need to call the Port Authority and Coast Guard. Let me know if you find anything more on Boris and Mikail."

"I will." Ricardo ended the call.

Hamilton turned toward Tessa.

"I need to go. I have the name of a ship that Ray may be on, and I need to check in at the office. You stay here."

"Do I look like I'm going anywhere?"

"You look great, considering."

"What, considering I probably had a nervous breakdown, froze myself in the tub, and cried all the tears my body can muster? Please."

I'll call you," he said as he stepped out the door.

# # #

Tessa stood, drew the hotel curtain back slightly, and watched Hamilton walk to his car. Then she picked up her cell phone and dialed her mother.

The phone rang twice, then she heard, "Hello," followed by a clicking sound. *What is up with this hotel phone?* Her chest tightened as her thoughts raced through the possibilities.

"Mom? Did you hear that?"

"Tessa? Hear what?"

"That clicking sound."

"I didn't hear anything clicking. How are you doing with our Agent Hamilton?"

"He just left. Something about the ship Ray might be on." She sat, started doodling on the pad by the hotel phone.

"How are you holding up? Do you want us to come over?"

She chewed on her lower lip. "I'm struggling. No, don't come. It's a mess... I'm a mess."

"Wait, what? What mess?"

"Mom, I can't even explain what's happened." She tore off a scribbled page, tossed it, missing the trash can, and began to doodle again.

"You and Agent Hamilton?" Mom's voice held a note of accusation.

"No, Mom, are you kidding? No...nothing... Mother, stop."

The clicking sound returned.

"There, did you hear that?"

"Sorry, dear, I only hear your voice."

Tessa pulled back the curtain again and peeked out to the parking lot. A woman with a dog walked by, and a few cars moved past the hotel.

She tried to recall the conversation, the advice from Hamilton. Calls and the ability of these kidnappers to track her down. Her stomach began to ache. "Mom, I should probably go."

"Are you sure we shouldn't come?"

"No, I'm fine. Agent Hamilton will be coming back soon, I'm sure."

"OK, but we're both worried terribly about you."

"I'll call you later." She ended the call.

25

The gray haze thinned to a blue hue, and the salty air blew cooler, whipping the torn Russian flag on the stern of the ship. Captain Konstantin Semenov, hands tight on the old iron wheel, steered straight away from the coast of America. Leonid Kotov, the second officer, waited to take command of the *Arisha* and scanned the horizon for any crossing vessels. The twanging sound of feet stomping on steel stairs resonated over the rumbling of diesel engines. Vladislav Mishkin entered the bridge through the side steel door, clanging as it closed behind him.

"I will not go to America jail on the account of you taking this man," Captain Semenov boldly stated, standing stiffly at the helm.

"Relax. Two-hundred miles to safety, maybe five hours," Vladislav responded, sipping fresh, steaming coffee from a dark ceramic mug.

"I will only relax when he and his cargo is off my ship."

"What do you know of his cargo?"

Semenov removed his captain's hat, brushed it against his leg and set it back on his head. "They said beautiful jewels, strange jewels, and shiny metal objects."

"Who says of these things?"

Semenov furrowed his brow. "I won't tell. You and your promise of money to hold secrets does not work on captained ship at sea. I ask of my crew, and they tell me these things."

Vladislav lifted his cup to his lips and took a sip. "Hopefully we can get good money for them, pay for *Arisha* repairs." He lifted his cup in a gesture of success.

"Leonid, *vy seichas berete comando na vakhtu.*" Captain Semenov instructed his second officer to take the watch command. The tall, lean Leonid saluted, stepped forward, and placed a hand on the large wheel.

"I called my father. He is most pleased, but I sense worry also. My dead brother, his body on its way to Moscow. I'm afraid they will bury him before Mr. Holland."

Seminov faced the oncoming sea, pulled gently on his beard and narrowed his eyes. "Why do you tell me this? My only concern is safe travel to Vladivostok, and the crew paid."

"Don't worry about your crew. They will be paid. My father assures me."

"He owns this ship, but without cargo, we only waste time and money. Our agent here was to provide a cargo of salt. In our rush to leave, we have nothing. Now how will he pay?"

"Ah, you forget, we have cargo. We have Holland. I only wish I had his wife, also."

"He is not cargo; he is only trouble. You will see." Captain Semenov waved his hand over his head and stepped through the side door off the bridge.

"*Kak pozhivaet nash gost?*" Vladislav asked the second officer regarding the status of Ray Holland.

Leonid explained he was alive, had eaten one meal, and remained in the stern hold.

Vladislav expressed his appreciation for keeping tabs on Holland, instructing him to move him to Georgiy's old quarters when they made two hundred miles.

Leonid offered a nod in response. Vladislav glared, turning only after receiving a smile.

# # #

Leonid watched as Vladislav moved across the helm controls, flipping two switches. He pretended not to notice when Vladislav disabled the Automatic Identification System, which sent ship information to satellites and ground stations. It was used to alert other ships in the area to avoid collisions. Vladislav slowly walked to the gray steel side door of the bridge, stepping to the stairwell without a word.

Leonid quickly called his captain's quarters from the bridge phone, alerting him of the change. Captain Semenov voiced annoyance with the gesture of his first officer but let it go. He instructed Leonid to turn it back on at the two-hundred-mile distance, and definitely before dark.

26

Footsteps clomped. Ray snapped his head up. *Not someone trying to be quiet.* An unfamiliar dark silhouette appeared in the lighted doorway of the dark, cavernous place he was being held. A man too tall, too thin to be Vladislav. The image grew larger as he approached. The lamp Angelina provided had grown dimmer, providing only limited sight now of the food she provided him and the towel for his swollen temple.

"Who are you?" Ray asked.

"Leonid my name." He untied Ray from the chair. The pain lessened in his chest, and he was able to breathe easier. Leonid lifted him by his forearm to a stand and held him, allowing him to gain his balance on his one good leg.

Ray asked, "Where are we going?"

"Sorry, no English."

"I don't know Russian," Ray admitted, then asked, "Angelina?"

Leonid glanced at him, then shrugged. Slowly, he moved him toward the doorway into the bright passageway.

Ray lifted his hand to his forehead, squinting. After navigating a challenging staircase, they arrived in a small room with a bunk bed. A simple metal table sat against the wall, with a woven cloth chair next to it. Leonid helped him into the soft chair.

He sighed. A pleasant relief from the painful several minutes of his foot cast striking every outcropping in the narrow passageways of the old ship. Leonid opened a small white refrigerator on the floor, checking its contents. It contained bottles of water, red cans with the familiar Coke logo, and three dark bottles resting on top.

Leonid grabbed one held it, then placed in his jacket pocket. He stepped over to a second doorway in the room, opened it, and looked at Ray to make sure he saw the toilet, sink, and shower.

Not knowing much about maritime life, he figured this must be an officer's quarters to include such luxuries, particularly on this old ship. Despite peeling paint, rust, broken and missing handles on doorways, these quarters were clean and neat.

"Angelina *budet ryadom, chtoby pozabotitsya au vas.*" Leonid stood in the doorway, then he shut the door.

Ray understood the name Angelina, and figured he must have said something to the effect she would be by, but he had no idea. Exhausted, ready to relieve himself, he took advantage of the bathroom. Then he crawled across the room to the lower bed and rested his head on the soft, fresh-smelling pillow. He quickly went to sleep despite the bright light from the incandescent bulb's glow in the center of the ceiling.

27

Angelina knelt in front of a four-drawer mahogany wood dresser, digging through her blouses, sweatshirts, pants, and undergarments. Picking up each item, she held it in front of her nose, giving it a whiff. Then she put the items needing washing in one pile, and everything else went back into the dresser she shared with Vladislav. She heard the door handle turn, and it pushed open. Not expecting anyone, she jumped back. Vladislav stepped in, a look of surprise on his face.

"What are you doing?" He shut the door behind him.

"Sorting my clothes for washing. They all smell of this ship, these musty drawers."

"Why do you care how you smell on this ship? It only matters to me really."

Angelina frowned, said nothing.

"It's no matter." He sat on a padded wooden chair. "I am troubled. It seems Mikail was unable to take Holland's wife. But says he will try again."

"Why not just leave her?" She put her selected soiled garments into a white fabric sack with a drawstring.

"Don't tell Holland of this matter. He needs to remain concerned."

"How would you even get her on board now that we are at sea?"

"Mikail has means to move people to and from Russia."

Angelina furrowed her brow. "Like those children in his home?"

Vladislav pounded his fist on the table next to him and howled, "You are not to speak of these things. I won't hear of it any longer."

"So, it disgusts you?" She paused, watching him as he appeared to contemplate his feelings. "That is good," she continued. "Is Holland to do something with the beautiful stones, what they can do?"

"Yes, yes."

"How can he in the dark hold? He cannot do anything tied to a chair."

"Leonid has moved him to quarters now. What do you know of him?"

"There are no secrets on this ship, you even say such things."

"You should stay away from him."

She clenched her fist, her body tensed. "Then you should tell him what you want."

"I will ask Leonid to do."

"Leonid knows no English, how can he?"

Vladislav growled. "I will tell him then."

"And strike him again? That will not help." She pursed her lips. Careful not to push him hard enough for a violent reaction.

"What then?"

"Let me."

He gave her a piercing look, then rose to his feet. Roughly, he took hold of her arm and jerked her close, pressing his cheek against hers. "If he touches you, he dies."

Her face flushed hot. "And your father, what of his desire to avenge Viktor?

He pushed her away. "I will apologize. He will understand."

"He dies, you will never know of his device, its power."

Vladislav turned around, opened a cabinet, grasped a dark bottle and empty glass, and poured himself a generous portion of Russian whiskey. He held the bottle up. "You want some?"

"Yes."

He pointed to the cabinet. "Get your own glass."

Scowling, Angelina stepped over, pulled out a tall clear glass, and set it in front of Vladislav. After he poured, he surprised her by wrapping his free arm around her waist, spinning her around, and planting a passionate kiss on her lips.

She gently pushed him away and took a sip of her whiskey.

Still holding her, he said, "I would have you stay for sex, but I am on watch now. Maybe after."

Angelina smirked, peeled his hand from her side, and tipped the remainder of the whiskey into her mouth, slapping the glass on the counter.

Vladislav smiled. "Impressive."

"So, I will tell Holland of the need to show the device and its power to you before we arrive in Vladivostok?"

"Yes, yes. Have Leonid help you also." He waved his hand over his head. "I must go." He turned and stepped out the cabin door.

28

Ray opened his eyes, unsure how long he'd slept, and stared at the bunk bed above. The smell of seared meat, potatoes, sweet corn, and fresh bread awakened his senses. Turning his head, he recognized the shapely curve of Angelina's bottom in dark blue jeans, leaning over the single metal table in his quarters. He smiled, knowing his seemingly only friend on this ship was nearby. The only person on the ship who so far spoke any English besides Vladislav, the man who wanted to kill him.

She turned and smiled when she noticed his eyes open. "I am so glad Leonid moved you. Much better than that dark cold place." She stood after straightening the tray of food. Ray smiled, sat up, and groaned momentarily from his muscle spasming chest.

"Angelina, you realize I will need to crawl over there unless you help me."

"Of course, I will help." She grinned, stepped around a chair, and took him under the arm, lifting him easily. Her strength surprised Ray, expecting he would need to pull himself to a stand. Sitting, he looked up at her as she swept her long bleached-blonde straight hair from her face. Then he noticed the top two buttons of her knit blouse unbuttoned, showing off cleavage. Probably not meant to be seen by the crew. He looked away, trying to hide the obvious.

Turning his attention back to his tray of food, he said, "I feel I need to meet this ship's cook. You said his name was Dominique?"

"Maybe possible, but he knows no English."

"If I shake his hand and smile, will he understand that?"

"Yes." She held her finger to her lips, stepped over to the door to his quarters, and closed it gently.

She whispered, "Sorry to say, but Vlad speaks of taking your wife."

Ray spit out his partly chewed bread. "What, why?" he snarled.

"Shh, you must keep quiet."

"Sorry, but why does he need Tessa?" Irritation pricked at his chest like pins and needles.

"I think a prize for his father most, but he speaks of your stones also. He wants to know more. He wants you to show him."

Ray shook his head and pondered while taking a bite of the diced, well-buttered potatoes. What was there to show Vladislav? Impressive would be the power of the original first and second projects.

He had spent months since the accident that killed Viktor re-engineering his GG-named project. GG came from the term Gravity Gone, so named when the stones first reacted to an electrical charge, floating freely on his desk. The stones were now set in a mesh array with a low voltage charge applied, the stones' orientation being critical. He'd finally come to the conclusion that the earth's magnetic field provided a relational response to the stone's powers and determined flight direction. Lift came in correlation to earth's gravitational force. His device now was about the size of a stack of regulation sized frisbees.

Unfortunately, getting the house ready for a baby and the pressures at his job at Laubner Labs on the fusion laser development had slowed his progress. But this smaller device's force capability wouldn't be impressive enough to save anybody, even Tessa.

"Angelina, I'm afraid the device wouldn't impress him, even if I could make it fly."

"You said levitate before. What you do you mean, fly?"

Given his situation, Ray realized there was no point in keeping any of this secret. It wouldn't matter in a couple weeks, but Tessa was innocent of any wrongdoing. Her life was worth saving.

"Levitate and flight are the same," he tried to explain. "My first device flew uncontrolled across the sky. The second device dug a hole. What remains is much smaller in scale."

"Scale?" She cocked her head.

"Less force." Angelina stared at him and placed a finger to her chin.

"You understand force?" he asked.

"Yes." Furrowing her brow, she squatted, leaned in, and placed her hand gently on his. "I understand force. How much is force?"

"It's complicated." Knowing she wouldn't understand the physics of the fusion force generated power, he tried to offer a simpler explanation. "I'm guessing two hundred pounds."

Patting his arm repeatably, she smiled, revealing a missing premolar from her lower jaw.

"My weight, one-twenty-five, I need to understand more. How can I help?"

Help me? Why help me? It was Vladislav who's controls my fate. Tessa's freedom would only come by a successful demonstration. Unless Angelina… She touched his hand breaking his thought.

"Can you bring me my devices and stones?" he asked, understanding it unlikely without some sort of supervision.

She hesitated. "I will tell Leonid. He will tell Vlad, so you will need to show him."

He wondered if she needed to be careful of her involvement with anything to do with him. It made sense that Leonid would be involved. The result would provide Vladislav what he wanted. If this would save Tessa, it was worth it, but he wondered if he could trust Angelina or if she had a plan of her own.

29

Ray crawled on the dull gray vinyl floor between the two white two-gallon buckets containing his fusion stones, almost spilling one. As the trip toward Russia reached its third day, he felt an urgent need to showcase the stones' power to Vladislav and potentially spare Tessa from abduction. Although out to sea, he wondered how Vladislav would be able to do anything to Tessa unless he had connections in the Bay Area. Maybe drug her and put her on a plane. *Angelina has her passport though.* He remembered her taking it from their home. This could impact Vladislav's ability to get her out of the country.

He still couldn't risk it. Situated in the belly of this rusty ship, he needed to focus on what he could do. Right now, being able to walk, or even hobble with a cane, would be beneficial. His other challenge was having his old GG housing – the size of a truck tire – in his quarters, taking up valuable space. It would be better off at the bottom of the ocean with his other GG device. The integrated DC power supply and circuit board would be the only components of use.

His current project's housings were made of hard alloy, in the shape of a donut. After taking an inventory, he needed a few simple tools to hurry things along. A calculator, multi-tester, solder, iron, and his laptop. The laptop was a problem. Apparently, that was not one of the items taken from his Palo Alto home. Could he make the adjustments accurately without all the data he'd collected prior? He doubted it. He was back to square one, performing tests and collecting data, which, inside a moving ship made of steel, could be disastrous.

A gentle knock came at the door to his quarters. Angelina appeared, wearing black spandex pants and a tight pink top, accompanied by a familiar scent. It was one of Tessa's favorite perfumes, "Happy" by Clinique, one of the things she had removed from their home.

Standing tall, she looked down. "Why are you on floor?"

Ray chucked. "If I had a cane or crutches, I could hobble around."

"What is hobble?"

"Never mind. Can you get me a cane or crutches, like I had at my home? It could speed this along."

Angelina said nothing for a moment, then suddenly responded, "Yes." Reaching down, she grasped his arm, lifting him up, and helped him into a chair at his small metal table. A jolt of energy ran through his entire body with the prospect of walking better. He contemplated asking about the removal of the big GG housing. He had already removed the two necessary components, so it seemed unnecessary to keep it. Angelina, who had been making regular appearances twice a day, appeared to be eager to assist. He wondered if she had received permission from Vladislav to help with his care. He smirked. *I doubt it.*

Glancing up at her blue eyes, long blond hair draped over her ample breasts, he said, "That would be great. Do you think you can get this returned to wherever it came from?" He pointed toward the large GG housing.

"Yes. Leonid can come."

Unsure if Angelina could translate the listed needs to Leonid, he wrote them down on a small five-inch yellow tablet, then handed it to her. Using both hands to take the note, she held his hand for a moment to read it. "How soon will you show Vlad?"

"I'm not sure. Depends on getting those items."

Her gaze dropped, and she released his hand. Squatting, she leaned in so close he could see the short blond hairs on her chin and upper lip.

"You must show soon. You are smart, went to university. You must show before we arrive to Vladivostok." A tear formed in her right eye, which she wiped away.

Moved by her insistence, the reason confused him. Ray placed his hands on her shoulders and pulled her gently in, hugging her. She wrapped her arms tight around his neck.

"Angelina. Get me these things on the list, and I will show Vlad before we arrive in Vladivostok."

She turned her head, kissed his temple, holding her lips there for a long moment. She stood, wiped another tear, and then smiled.

"I will tell Vlad if he cannot get, then no show. This will help. I must go." She turned and hurried out the door.

Ray hoped he'd bought some time, but his thoughts of Angelina were becoming too tempting to not take serious care. But she was Vladislav's girlfriend, a man who had no issue striking or humiliating him. A chill ran through his body. Anything appearing personal between them could bring a quick end to his and possibly her life.

30

The sky darkened and evening drew near. Agent Hamilton frowned as he sat next to CIA Officer Jeff Ricardo in his white Ford van.

"I'm not liking conducting this surveillance in the dark." Hamilton shuffled in his seat. "We should put someone inside."

Officer Ricardo glanced at him. "You were the one who didn't want to tell Mrs. Holland we were here after the hit on her phone."

Hamilton appreciated the fact that Officer Ricardo's team was able to get the cell phone provider to monitor and track her calls. They caught a break when a call to her parents' home was intercepted, and a third party was picked up tracking the call. It had been traced to an empty warehouse in downtown San Francisco just four city blocks from the Russian Consulate. A CIA team was preparing to enter the warehouse this same evening.

Hamilton placed his big hand on the dash and twisted to loosen a tight back muscle. "He better come soon, or I'll call this off and pull her out of there."

"You have the picture I sent you? Check this guy out." Ricardo pointed to a man stepping out of a gray Dodge Caravan. He pulled the printed picture out of his jacket, glanced at it, then gazed back at the man as he stood at the passenger door talking to someone in the van with the window down. "Looks like him."

"Somebody else in the van." Ricardo pointed out.

"What are they doing?" Hamilton squinted through the windshield.

"He's got something in his hand, some sort of device."

"Tracking her phone probably. That means he knows what room she's in. We need to go, right now." Hamilton pulled out his Glock 23, checked it, and released the safety.

"Hold on, we need them both. I don't want a car chase. Tuck that away, and we'll casually make our way toward them."

Hamilton set the safety back on, stuck the pistol back into his shoulder holster, and rested his hand on the door handle.

"Let's go." Ricardo opened the car door, stepping out to the front of the van. Hamilton joined him. They walked across the parking lot toward the main entrance, then turned toward the Caravan parked on the side lot. Mikail Sokolov was studying the hotel, apparently trying to gauge the layout orienting it to his cellular signal tracker. A head popped out of the passenger window, glancing at them.

"That's Boris. We've been spotted," Ricardo said softly. Mikail looked back, saw the two men coming toward them, and bolted toward the front of the Caravan. Hamilton and Ricardo charged, each pulling out their service weapons.

Hamilton yelled, "FBI," as he pointed his Glock at Mikail who ignored them both. Hamilton wanted this to end here and now and kept charging as the taller man pulled the car door open. Sokolov had one leg inside the van when Hamilton body-slammed him against the car door. He screamed when his leg snagged against the seat. They both bounced off the door as it angrily pushed back. Hamilton twisted, and Mikail fell to the ground face down.

Holding him down, Hamilton glanced into the van, seeing a wide-eyed Boris staring at Officer Ricardo's Glock pointed at his head from outside the open window. The officer opened the door and quickly pulled Boris to the ground.

After searching the men, Hamilton found a switchblade knife on Mikail, as well as a small bottle of chloroform and a handkerchief. They found no weapons in the van, which looked to have been stolen, since it contained a package of diaper wipes, a child seat, and some size four rubber boots in the back. The cellular signal tracker lay smashed on the ground next to the vehicle.

Once both men were cuffed and hooded in the back of the CIA van, Hamilton dialed 911 and reported the discovery of the possible stolen vehicle.

"I'm taking these two to HQ for interrogation, then I'll pass them onto the county jail," Ricardo said. "You'll need to file the federal charges for the kidnap attempt. Our investigation is ongoing, but there may be child sex trafficking and drug charges to add to the list."

Hamilton brushed off his jacket. "The work has only just begun."

"You can tell Mrs. Holland she can go home now at least."

"I will, but if you find anything else about other parties involved in this, you'll let me know, correct?"

"Of course."

31

The *Arisha* lifted and fell across building waves in the Pacific Ocean, now halfway to Vladivostok. Captain Semenov stood watch on the bridge, reading weather reports, verifying against what he recognized of the current sea and sky. His stomach felt rock hard as the image of his ship rolling out of control crossed his mind. Relieving his second officer, Leonid Kotov, he reviewed the log entries regarding other ship traffic and the noticeable building of the sea state. The wind speed and direction indicated a cold front was approaching.

Of particular note was the chief engineer reporting concerns of an overheating issue in the engine room and the need to slow the ship to find the cause. With comments regarding several failed gauges, he was struggling to trace cooling issues of the large diesel engines. Semenov feared the possible consequences of slowing the ship against the building waves. At his current speed, he could keep the ship at a proper angle of the rolling sea to maintain comfort for his crew. Otherwise, a new course away from the approaching storm was in order.

Suddenly lights flashed on the console concerning the starboard engine; it had lost power. The black phone on the wall, cracked from age and exposure, chimed. Semenov picked it up. It was his chief engineer, reporting the starboard engine was shut down because of a cooling failure.

"*Kak skoro ispravit?*" he asked how long to repair.

Semenov moved the phone from his ear because of the loud commotion of screaming, arguing, and yells from the crew and Chief Engineer Sergei Bychkov, often referred to as a stumpy old man of the sea. Bychkov apologized to his captain for the outburst, assuring him he would find a solution quickly.

With the starboard engine off, the ship began turning to port, exposing it to more broadside strikes from the building waves. The ship vibrated with each strike. Semenov rotated the ship's wheel to compensate, but it was clear the power wasn't sufficient. Another wave struck, causing the ship to turn even more to port. He adjusted and turned south, relenting to the power of the sea and the weak state of his ship. Yelling down to Bychkov over the phone, trying to drown out the continued shouts in the background, he let him know they were turning away from the storm, seeking calmer waters. Then he hung up.

His junior officer, Denis Elin, stumbled through the door, falling forward as the ship rocked. He'd once been an English teacher before taking the merchant marine position because of the promised pay.

"Captain," he yelled, trying for a salute while bracing himself, and crawling to a stand. "What happened?"

"Starboard engine is off, a cooling issue."

"Sir, what can we do?" His eyes were as wide as saucers.

"We must show calm, or we make things worse for us," Semenov reassured his young officer. Although well educated, Elin had little experience at sea. Now he was being tested on a ship in need of repair in an unforgiving ocean.

Semenov ordered, "Take the wheel, hold this heading. Storm is moving west. We will head south to calmer seas. We will be fine."

Elin took the wheel from his captain, grasping it more firmly than needed, and spread his skinny legs for balance. Semenov smiled and placed his captain's hat on the young sailor's nearly shaved head.

Before adding notes to the log on the console, he picked up the phone again to request more speed from Sergei to handle the rolling seas. His response was a resounding "No," explaining the port engine was now showing signs of overheating.

Suddenly, a wave crashed over the stern of the ship, causing a hoist to bend and sway dangerously on the aft deck.

"Ty "slyshish'? vy "vot pochemu nam nuzhno bol'she skorosti," Semenov yelled into the phone, alerting him to the conditions, and the reason they needed more speed.

Sergei apologized but cautioned about the danger of doing so.

Semenov was aware of the danger - not being able to maneuver in the current sea conditions could have serious consequences. He watched his junior officer struggle to hold the southerly heading.

"We must do what we must do," he instructed Elin.

"Aye, sir."

Two hours passed, the sea now ten-foot breaking waves instead of twenty. Elin was able to hold course, although he was ready for a break. Semenov left the bridge to gain a closer examination of the situation in the engine room and to calm the nerves of his crew.

# # #

The main bridge door creaked as it opened. Vladislav Mishkin stood, one hand on the wall, his face pale, almost matching his yellowing blond hair. "Where is captain?" he asked, his free hand covering his mouth, holding back a belch.

Elin straightened his captain's hat. "He went below to check on the starboard engine. You don't look well."

"I'm not, no thanks to operation of this ship."

"I'm afraid it is the sea..." Elin removed a hand from the wheel and pointed toward the bow of the ship.

"Silence," Vladislav shouted then covered his mouth. Another sour belch spoiled the surrounding air. "I can't go below. I must stay up here for now."

"Good, you can take watch. Focusing on the handling of the ship will help your seasickness."

"I never get seasick," Vladislav grumbled.

"I'm afraid many do under the right conditions. You are the first officer, so please relieve me, sir."

"Yes, yes, you're relieved. If you see captain, tell him I have watch."

"Aye aye, sir." Elin saluted and made a quick entry in the log as Vladislav grasped the helm. Elin let him know the current course heading, then left the bridge.

A short time later, a voice came from the bridge entrance. Vladislav jumped.

"I hear you are not well?" Semenov asked the still pale Vladislav.

"I'm fine."

"I wondered about you during our situation. I gave lone watch to Elin so I could attend to our engine issues."

"I don't get seasick," Vladislav interrupted.

"You look it."

"I'm feeling better."

"Not for long." The captain chuckled wryly.

"What now?"

Semenov lifted a coffee mug from the counter, looked inside, frowned. "We must shut down both engines for repairs at sea. The conditions will take us toward the US Hawaiian Islands, maybe two or three days. It will be shameful to be rescued by American Coast Guard if we approach shore limits."

"Better that than go aground." He pointed to the empty pot on the coffee maker.

Semenov clunked the cup back onto the counter. "I will not let that happen. I will call Dimitri Mishkin to see of any ships nearby and complain of his ship's poor condition."

"I will call for you," Vladislav insisted.

"Go, do so now. Come back and tell me status. I will take watch."

32

A rich orange glow painted the west bedroom wall of the Holland home. Tessa lay face up, staring at the ceiling, a pile of used tissues next to her. Against her parents' wishes, she wanted to be in her own home, awaiting possible word on Ray. And to mourn in private the loss of her baby girl. Her mother calling every couple of hours didn't help her lack of sleep, nor preparing anything to eat. The phone rang. Reluctantly, she picked it up, knowing it was her mother again.

"Tessa, are you decent?" she asked.

"Mom, what kind of question is that?" She sat up, glanced at her reflection in the full-length mirror mounted on the wall, and frowned.

"Oh-so-special Agent Bryce Hamilton was here looking for you," Mom cooed.

"At this hour?" She looked for her watch that was nowhere to be found.

"Tessa, it's almost 8:30," she paused. "I wish I would have known he was coming. I would have put on something nice to wear, baked a Danish."

"Mother, you're married, remember?"

"I know. He's so handsome though. Anyway, he's on his way to see you."

"What?" she screamed. "How long ago?"

"Oh, no worries. He's still here talking to your father in the driveway."

"Mom, keep him there as long as you can." She glanced toward her walk-in closet, clothes still on the floor. Her dresser was at least more in order – underwear, some blouses folded and put away.

"I'll do my best, but he just got in his car and started the engine."

"Mom," she yelled. "Every time I see him, I'm a mess. I need a shower, my hair. He'll be here in fifteen minutes."

"I'll do my best."

Tessa hung up, leaped off the messy bed, and sprinted to the bathroom.

Applying a rich rouge lipstick while leaning into the bathroom mirror, still sweating from shower steam, she recognized the crunching sound of tires on gravel. He was there. Able to find a knee-length skirt that didn't need ironing, a too-sheer beige button-up blouse, she ran to the closet for shoes. Flats will have to do. After slipping on a pair of blue canvas sneakers, she took one last look in the mirror, and drew a deep breath. Maybe a sweater to throw over her top; her nipples were too apparent. Okay for Ray, but for anyone else, this would be improper. The doorbell chimed. It was too late.

"Coming!" she yelled, trampling down the hall, turning, almost falling down the first step of their steep, narrow staircase. She felt her heart beat hard at the possibility.

Opening the door, there he was, those bright blue eyes, a gleaming white smile. She blushed.

"I thought you were staying with your parents."

"Oh, I changed my mind, woman's prerogative, you know." She couldn't believe she just said that.

Still smiling, he asked, "May I come in?"

"Yes, of course." She stepped back, holding the door open. "Please excuse the mess. I haven't had enough time to get this all cleaned up."

"That's understandable." He glanced at her as she shut the door, giving her a once over, and stopped an uncomfortable moment staring at her blouse. "You look great."

Tessa turned her body, trying to hide the obvious. "Thanks. Can I get you something?"

"Coffee? he asked. "I've been non-stop all morning."

"I can do that. Just give me a couple minutes." She walked into the kitchen. "Why are you here?" she yelled while running water into her coffee maker.

"You don't need to yell," he said, standing tall in the narrow doorway of the kitchen.

"Oh, sorry." Her face warmed.

"I'm afraid I have some good news and bad news." His voice held no emotion.

Tessa's mouth dropped open. "Ray?" she inquired softly.

"No. I'm afraid Ray is neither part of the good news nor bad. We are involved in a local manhunt, which is occupying a large portion of my time. Certainly, having the two that tried to kidnap you in jail now takes some of the pressure off."

"What about my husband? What happens now?" She turned away and stared out the kitchen window.

"Well, this is part of the good news. I'm applying more time to your case, but unofficially. This means I'm limited when it comes to the resources of the FBI."

The coffee dribbled into the freshly rinsed pot. Tessa grabbed two cups from the dish drainer on the counter.
"You came all this way just to tell me this, or is there something else?"

"Actually, there is. I have the FBI reports on the Viktor Mishkin kidnapping, and I reached out to our friends in the CIA. Viktor is the son of a Dimitri Mishkin in Moscow. I was provided a large file on him, but I caught a break when I received information regarding his ownership of a small fleet of merchant ships. *Afina, Arisha,* and *Allia. Allia* is currently docked in Vladivostok, Russia. *Afina* is in the north Pacific, destination unknown, and *Arisha*'s most recent port was San Francisco Bay. So, I speculate *Arisha* must be where your husband is. I requested the Coast Guards' help in tracking this ship. I just heard from their Hawaii station, she is eighty miles north of Oahu and has altered coarse and slowed."

"What does that mean?"

"Actually, I see it as an opportunity, for two reasons. If they sail into US Waters, the Coast Guard will have jurisdictional rights to board them. If they are outside US waters having some sort of mechanical issues, then the Coast Guard may lend assistance and likely board the vessel. If Ray is there, they'll find him. The other opportunity was to ask the Coast Guard to go immediately and investigate. I put in the request but received pushback on that. Although they did assure me they are sending one of their Lockheed HC-130 turboprop aircraft to get in contact. I should hear something before noon today."

"Hear something about Ray?" She poured coffee into his cup.

"No, I would only hear if the *Arisha* acknowledged contact and were receptive to assistance if needed. If they accept assistance, then a cutter would be sent, or maybe a marine tug."

"We wait?"

"Actually, no." He sipped the hot coffee too quickly and coughed.

Tessa grabbed a napkin and dabbed the coffee drip on his chin. Agent Hamilton gently grasped her hand holding the tissue and held it to his chin. "We're going to Hawaii."

Tessa let go of the napkin, retracted her hand, and froze. Unable to comprehend what was unfolding before her, her stomach churned, her heart raced, and the room spun. She desperately wished for someone to embrace her and help her through all of this. Now this handsome, capable man was taking charge, leading the way, probably risking his job for her. *He wants to take me to Hawaii to rescue my husband!*

She made an effort to clear her thoughts. She was married. As mad as she was at Ray, he was still her husband. Tessa glanced at the napkin on the floor, and they both bent to pick it up. In that moment, their faces drew close. Agent Hamilton smiled.

Tessa stood abruptly, spun around, and hurriedly left the kitchen, saying, "I have to use the bathroom, please excuse me."

Staring at her image in the old bathroom mirror that needed re-silvering in the corners, she saw her flushed neck, her all-too-apparent clinging blouse. With nothing to cover her exposed top, she stepped out of the bathroom, and rushed up the stairs to her bedroom. On her hands and knees, she dug through her button sweater tops until she found one, shook the wrinkles out, and put it on. Looking at herself in the mirror, she made a quirky frown before going downstairs to find the agent halfway through his coffee at the kitchen table.

"Sorry about that," he said.

"Sorry about what?"

"You changed?"

She looked down. "Oh this, I was just cold."

"I noticed." He smiled.

She was afraid of that. Afraid she had forgotten all about the overexposure, probably giving him the wrong message. Too late now. She tried to think of something to say, then, "When are we leaving?"

"Tomorrow, 8:10am, United Airlines, first-class. I'll pick you up."

"Shit," she burst out. "Oh sorry, I just...need to pack. How long –?"

"Just pack light," he interrupted. "We can buy clothes if we stay too long. The hotel also has laundry services."

Almost afraid to ask, she whispered, "Hotel room?" blushing.

"Two connected rooms, so I'm right there if you need me."

Excited to go to Hawaii, having never been, she remained shocked by the confusion of her thoughts. What happens in Hawaii while traveling with this attractive undercover FBI agent? Does she sit in the hotel while he risks his life and job to save her husband? The same man she'd like to punch for putting her through all this.

The phone rang, interrupting her scrambled thoughts. She picked up the receiver, "Hello?"

Her mother-in-law jumped right in. "Can I talk to Ray?"

Tessa placed her hand over the mouthpiece of the phone and whispered to the agent, "Ray's mother. She doesn't know about him."

"Debra, Ray isn't here. Didn't the police come by to see you?"

Agent Hamilton stood and pointed toward his cell phone as he pulled it from his jacket pocket. He walked into the living room.

"Debra, I'm so sorry no one has been by, but Ray is in trouble." She glanced at her shoes, not sure what to disclose to Ray's frail mother. She couldn't bring to mind any words that would soothe her. And now about to head to Hawaii, maybe rescue Ray, maybe not.

Agent Hamilton stepped back into the kitchen and reached for the phone in Tessa's hand. She hesitated, then handed it over.

"Mrs. Holland, this is Special Agent Bryce Hamilton with the FBI. We are actively looking for your son, who was taken from his home. We're following several leads and will know more soon. In the meantime, I have asked the Santa Clara Sheriff's Department to pay you a visit and keep you abreast of the situation and any updates. They should be there within the next half hour, so please stay home until they arrive."

A pause. "Mrs. Holland, do you understand? You stay there until the sheriff comes. He will help you and put you in contact with someone to help take care of your husband's memorial. I have to hang up now. Tessa and I need to go find Ray."

He disconnected the call.

"She's just going to call back," Tessa insisted.

Agent Hamilton picked up the receiver and placed it on the counter. "It'll ring busy."

"That's kind of rude, don't you think?"

"The sheriff will be there soon. They'll take care of your mother-in-law. You'll probably miss the memorial, though."

"I'm afraid if we don't find Ray, there'll be another. Debra's going to drink herself to death."

"I'm confident the sheriff's office and their support services will get her all taken care of."

She glanced into her empty coffee cup and reached for the pot. "I hope so. Her heart's in the right place. She just tries to drink stress away."

"I really need to go back to the office to check in on the manhunt we're on." He handed Tessa his empty cup.

She set it on the counter and followed him through the living room onto the front patio. He stopped and faced her, a little too close. Tessa knew this wasn't like a date; it was official FBI business. Why couldn't he just walk down the steps, go to his car, wave, and be gone? No, he couldn't continue without provoking her emotions once more. He reached out and grasped both her hands. She felt ready to be pulled in for a hug or something, but it didn't happen.

"We'll find Ray. Hell or high water, we'll find him." He released her hands after a gentle squeeze and shake. She felt a sinking sensation in her heart, followed by a sudden uplift. She couldn't tell which was right.

A moment later, he was gone.

33

After receiving all the items on the list given to Angelina two days earlier, Ray made progress despite the ship's heavy rocking. Now he was close to performing his first simple test. Angelina found him a large flashlight, removing the four D-sized batteries he needed. He soldered them in sequence to the redesigned power control board he had removed from his original GG device, now stored elsewhere on the ship. His fusion stones still bore markings indicating the magnetic directional orientation from previous experiments, which ultimately saved him valuable time.

The much smaller-scale device, using fewer stones, also saved time and space needed for testing. Using the meshed screen designed specifically for the size of the marble-like stones, he carefully placed them in the donut-shaped housing. Because of the rough seas, the ship's apparent loss of engines, and seasickness, he had to redo the placement three times. Fortunately, he found a bottle of fast-drying glue in a supply cabinet in his quarters, along with other items, including French porn magazines, cigarettes, and half a bottle of Double Black Johnny Walker Scotch. Successfully using the glue to hold the stones in place, the rocking ship was no longer a factor. At least in terms of assembly of the small test device, but the seasickness prevailed until Angelina brought him some Dramamine.

A knock came at the door. Angelina stood, this time in a mid-thigh skirt and over-sized T-shirt. Probably one of Vladislav's.

"There is too much yelling around Vlad. I need quiet." She stood still in the doorway, holding the door frame against the rocking. "American plane is flying around. Vlad says they are offering help. He said no. I wish he would say yes and get *Arisha* running."

"Does he know when they can repair and get back underway?" he asked, holding his small device steady on the table.

She ignored the question and peered at his hands steadying the metal housing, full now with the fluorescent stones.

"Is it ready, working?" She took two steps into his quarters and sat at the table across from him. She placed her hands on his and stared at the stones inside.

"Can you grab me the top?" He pointed to the floor, where most everything now lay, thanks to the rocking ship.

Releasing her grip on his hands, she steadied herself by placing one hand on the floor. She picked up the donut-shaped top with its matching holes to assemble the housing together and handed it to him. He placed it over the device, sealing the stones inside. Two wires hung down through roughly cut openings in the frames. The tips of the sturdy copper core wires had been exposed by the removal of their protective coverings. He pointed to the bolts in a small box, also on the floor. "Those too, please."

"You are so nice. Vlad never says please." She handed him the small box. "Are all American men nice to girlfriends?"

He placed the four bolts into each location, tightening them with his fingers, and securing the two halves, then looked up momentarily. "I mostly figure they are."

"Is this ready to work?" she asked, an eager look on her face.

"Yes and no."

She responded with a quizzical gaze.

"If my calculations are correct, we need to test it in a safe place, and someplace secure, so it doesn't move."

"I know just the place."

"You do?" He couldn't believe her quick response.

"Yes. I know a strong clamp, used for banging steel. Come, I will show you." She stood and tried to grasp his hand. He pulled it back to grab the soldered battery array and the donut-shaped device. He was careful not to make contact between the battery contacts and wires hanging out. He didn't want to take any chances, remembering the strong power of the stones from his prior three fusion stone events.

"Come, come," she insisted, still reaching for his full hands, grabbing his forearm instead. He pulled back, looking down at his cast. She covered her mouth with her hand and blushed. Stepping back, she reached around his waist, helping him take the weight off his slowly healing ankle.

They made slow progress out the cabin door, down the long passageway. Instead of taking the stairs, they used a freight elevator that ran on battery power from one of the diesel generators running on deck. If not for a working generator, the ship would be in worse shape than it was with both engines powered off.

She led him through a door, and it became evident they had entered a vast cargo hold. The space was immense, with a cavernous atmosphere that seemed to swallow the light. The air was damp, and the limited lighting only added to the mysterious ambiance. To the right was a small, lit doorway.

She pointed. "There."

Making it to the doorway, Ray noticed a large, heavily dented, oily table and two large, closed metal cabinets against one wall. Two huge vises were bolted and welded on each end of the table.

"Will this work?" She gestured to the one vise with her free hand.

Ray glanced at the floor, examining how it attached to the framing in the room. From the rocking, he felt they may be near the center of the ship, close to the waterline, which might suit his test. Still nervous about a possible failure, or event causing severe damage, what else could he do under the conditions? If it worked, he could show Vladislav and save his wife from harm. If it failed and killed him and Angelina, or sank the ship, Tessa would still be safe. He pointed his hand containing the battery assembly at the closer vise.

She held him tighter around the waist as they stepped toward it. He placed the battery assembly and fusion housing on the steel table and steadied himself as Angelina released him. She grabbed a wooden chair lying sideways on the floor. It was as greasy and dirty as the rest of the room, but he didn't care about his pants getting any dirtier, after all the previous crawling around he had done.

The ship's rolling had slowed over the last couple hours, but still rocked side to side twenty to thirty degrees. Angelina steadied herself against the dirty table. Brown and black grease now soiled her white skirt and T-shirt. Ray opened the vise, cranking on the large rod. As the ship rocked hard, Angelina's feet slipped, causing her to lose her grip on the fusion device and battery pack. She leaped across the table, her skirt lifting, providing Ray a clear look at her tiny pink panties. His face heated, and he tried to look away, but his attention was more on his device. Grabbing her thigh with both hands, he prevented her from sliding across the table.

She turned and gazed at him. "I have them."

As the ship righted again, she slid off the table. Ray let go of her thigh. She looked at his hands, then her thigh.

"You made me dirty." She smiled.

"Oh. What?" His face flushed hot again. He looked at his dirty hands, then at her smile. They both laughed. He blew out a sigh of relief that she had saved the two components from crashing to the floor, which would have certainly damaged the battery assembly. She held the donut-shaped device horizontal in the vise while he slowly cranked it closed. Putting as much torque as he could, he wrenched it tight and took a long breath.

Angelina grabbed another chair, dirtier than the one Ray sat in, and pulled it up close to him. She sat, spread her legs around his chair and legs, and scooted in closer. "Now ready?"

"Angelina. This could be dangerous. You understand, right?"

She frowned. "Yes, I understand danger."

He swiveled his head from side to side, to relieve nervous tension, then twisted the dark copper wire from the battery assembly to the fusion housing wire. Without a switch to use, he could only hold the second wire in place with his fingers. He gazed into her bright blue eyes, maybe for the last time. He rolled his shoulders, his nerves tingling.

Angelina smiled and rocked her head in response.

He pinched the remaining wires together, giving them a quick twist.

34

A thundering rumble echoed through the *Arisha*'s machine shop, and the lights flickered. As the room tilted forty degrees, Angelina's and Ray's bodies were thrown to the floor. Centrifugal forces began pulling them in the direction of the stern of the ship. Quick to wrap her long legs around Ray's waist, they grasped hold of a table leg. As the forces still pulled at them, he tried to quantify what was happening to the ship. The powered stones had moved, based on their magnetic alignment with the Earth's polarity. Now what? Were they headed back to San Francisco, the same result as two prior events? But they'd be dead if this were correct. And the ship's rocking had ceased, which was quite unusual.

"Oh, no." He twisted his body against the slippery floor. He grabbed for the hanging battery pack, slapping it with his hand, and snapped it free, breaking the wired connections. Immediately, they found themselves pressed hard to the floor, then suddenly lifted two feet into the air before crashing back down onto the steel floor.

Angelina landed atop him, her legs tight around his waist, arms wrapped around his neck. Ray wheezed from the flight, and

Angelina's firm body against him. His back burned like fire. He grimaced with pain.

"She gazed into his eyes. "What happened?"

"Too much force." He groaned.

"We show Vlad. He will be pleased."

"I'm not completely sure about that. I imagine most of the ship's crew are getting up off the floor like us. Hopefully, no one fell overboard."

"Hmmm." She sat upright atop him and placed a dirty finger to her cheek. "Why we not fly?"

"We did."

"No, no, why ship not fly?"

"Not enough force." He tried to sit up. Angelina didn't release her leg grip, so he propped himself on his elbows, despite his aching back. "We likely caused the ship to turn, and set it firm against the sea state, possibly pointed back to San Francisco. The captain will be confused about what just happened."

Angelina lifted her hand, about to place her finger on her cheek again. Noticing the grease, she laughed.
"I know I have not been to university, but you speak of force, enough force to move ship. Could this still move us, like you and me?"

Ray puzzled at the question momentarily. He pointed to her legs. Her face flushed as she released her vise grip. He sat up completely. Angelina stood, grasped his greasy hand, and lifted him onto his one good foot. Not sure how to respond yet to her question, he knew Vladislav and the ship's captain would want answers to what just happened. "Let's take this back to my room so I can think about your question."

Ray set the assembly on the lone table in his quarters and tried to wipe the grease off his hands with a paper towel. He gazed at his pants and shirt, appearing more like an oil worker than an engineer. Angelina's T-shirt didn't look so bad, although her legs were streaked, hands black, and a couple of grease prints dotted her face.

"I feel I need to get cleaned up." He pointed to the shower.

"Yes, me too." She smiled.

Ray pointed to the door. She shook her head.

"Angelina, I'm a married man. My back is on fire." He paused, relenting. "Soon to be a dead, married man." He glanced down.

She placed a finger on his chin, lifted it, and leaned in close. "I see something for your back." She gestured toward an open cabinet, the bottle of Johnny Walker Scotch on its side. She picked it up, grabbed two plastic cups from the sink, likely needing to be washed. "You're not dead yet."

"I will be if Vlad shows up, finding you in my shower."

She poured the two glasses half full. Giving up on trying to stand any longer, Ray sat on one of the wooden chairs. Angelina tipped her glass back, swallowing a strong mouthful, shook her head, and coughed once.

Ray took a sip from his glass, only his second of any hard alcohol – not since a junior high dance on a dare. He shook his head, coughed twice, then pinched his nose.

Angelina poured herself another half a glass, swirled it around, and downed it again in a single gulp. She sat.

Ray continued to take small sips, each tasting better. His awareness of the ship's movements came more easily with each swig. Soon, the fire in his back subsided.

"Feeling better?"

"Yes" He gave her a silly grin.

Angelina stood, causing her chair to slide, and placed her hand on the wall to steady herself from the ship's rocking and the effects of the scotch. Taking both hands, she lifted her T-shirt above her head, exposing her pale skin and bare chest.

Ray took another quick sip from his glass, then downed the rest.

Angelina grabbed the bottle, poured him another glass half full, then placed her hands on her hips and pushed down, dropping her short skirt to the floor, exposing nearly transparent pale pink bikini panties.

Ray swigged half his scotch and coughed again. Walking past him, running her finger across his shoulder, she dropped her panties before stepping into his quarters' head. She shut the door to prevent water from spraying into the room. Ray sat, stunned, pain softened by the alcohol. He tried to stand, but it was no use. Despite having a cast on his foot and feeling dizzy, he crawled to his bed and closed his eyes.

35

The horizon rocked back and forth as the merchant vessel *Arisha* lay sideways to the sea state. Although headed into the wind, she still drifted south toward Hawaii. Powered by one of the diesel generators on her aft deck, the display on the bridge was an array of blinking red. Calls continued to ring the wall-mounted phone, and wireless handsets were scattered about, squelching calls for help.

Captain Semenov was on the phone with his chief engineer Sergei Guzman who complained about his injured crew. Semenov was all too aware of injuries sustained when the *Arisha* rolled suddenly, followed almost immediately by the sixty-thousand-ton ship rising and falling. He'd wrapped his head hastily in a bandage from a bridge first aid kit, but blood soaked through. Semenov was on watch when the event occurred and had never experienced such a condition before. He shook his head, recalling the rolling six to eight-foot seas and fifteen to twenty knot winds. It was nothing special for this part of the ocean, but what happened was unanticipated. Still disabled, they were at the mercy of the conditions.

Now fifteen miles from US waters, with several injured crew, he was ready to request help from the US Coast Guard.

A squeak came as the bridge door opened. Vladislav stepped in with a slight limp, blood leaching through his long-sleeved, cotton gray-striped shirt.

"What happened here? I've been calling," Vladislav yelled.

"You think you are the only injured?" Semenov told his chief he would call back and hung up the phone. "I have several crew hurt. You, you brought this evil upon this ship." Semenov sneered as he braced a leg against the pedestal which held the wheel.

"Don't lay your 'God of the Sea' superstitions on me." Vladislav pointed at Semenov's stuffed black cat *Matros*, mounted on the wall.

"You explain then. I have seen storms do less damage. So many hurt, I am certainly to call American Coast Guard."

Vladislav slammed his foot down. "No... No American Coast Guard. Maybe If I throw our American guest into the sea, a tragic accident, then maybe. What do you know of your crew?"

"A broken arm, broken wrist, many concussions, cuts and bruises."

"What of you?"

"This is nothing, just a bump." Semenov waved his hand toward his head.

"Have all crew reported?"

"Yes, including your Angelina. She checked on your guest, he is bumped up, nothing bad."

Vladislav paused, scanned the horizon and the orientation of the ship to the sea. Drawing his hand to his chin, he shook his head.

"What?" Semenov asked.

"Nothing, it's just not possible."

"What?" he asked again. "If it concerns my ship, I need to know."

"It's not possible. I will check on Angelina and our guest myself."

"You are first officer. Your duty is to the ship. First you see to the needs of this ship and go find Leonid. Help him. He is in galley, then to forward holds assessing damage. *Arisha* must remain balanced."

Vladislav gazed again out the forward bridge windows and pointed at the slight list to starboard, the waves adding to the ship's lean. Bright lights appeared on the horizon. He stepped to the helm next to Semenov, grasped the bridge binoculars, and directed them toward the lights. "Here come our American friends again."

"If they see our state worse, they will send ships no matter what we say." Semenov glared at the approaching lights, trails of smoke following the Coast Guard plane.

"Even if they send ships, they cannot board us without our approval." Vladislav set the large binoculars back on the counter.

"Before our mishap, Sergei said one engine would work in one hour. Now he does not know. You must help Leonid."

A roar came from the four Allison T56-A-15 turboprop engines as the Lockheed HC-130 flew two hundred feet above the *Arisha*. The VHF radio on the bridge hissed, then a hail came on channel sixteen.

"US Coast Guard six-five-seven-niner, US Coast Guard six-five-seven-niner, US Coast Guard six-five-seven-niner calling freighter position twenty-five degrees twenty-two minutes north one-hundred-fifty-five degrees thirty-eight minutes west, do you read?"

Still braced against the bridge counter and wheel pedestal, Semenov picked up the radio and pressed to call. "This is *Arisha*, we read you, Coast Guard, over."

"*Arisha, Arisha, Arisha*, this is Coast Guard six-five-seven-niner. Are you in need of assistance, over?"

Semenov watched the HC-130 turn hard for another low pass. A couple of his crew were on the forward deck, waving. Picking up a corded handset off the bridge counter, he paged over the ship's audio system. "*Vernutsya na svoi stantsii*," he shouted, instructing them to return to their stations. Hanging up the page microphone, he resumed his response to the Coast Guard. "Coast Guard six-five-seven-niner, we do not need assistance, over."

"*Arisha*, this is Coast Guard six-five-seven-niner, switch to channel twenty-two, over."

Semenov twisted the dial to read twenty-two. The Coast Guard hailed again.

"*Arisha*, we show you drifting south. What is your condition, over?"

"Coast Guard, we have an overheat issue under repair. Fix is one hour, over."

"Roger that, *Arisha*. We are sending a vessel to you to stand by if you need assistance, over."

He growled before pressing the send button, not liking the dilemma Vlad had put his ship and crew in. Although the son of the owner yields power, Semenov was captain of the *Arisha*. "Understood, but we will be underway soon, over."

"*Arisha*, you have drifted far too long. You look to be listing. We should be on site in less than two hours, over."

"Roger, Coast Guard, *Arisha* out." He hung the microphone back on its clip. Then he picked up the phone and dialed the engine room. His chief answered.

"*U tebya yest' vsego dva chasa.*" Semenov told him he only had two hours, then ended the call.

36

As the United Airlines plane prepared to land in Hawaii, Tessa yawned to release the pressure in her ears during the plane's descent. Seated next to the window, she peered out, trying to catch a glimpse of Hawaii for the first time, although dense clouds were all she could see. Seated next to Agent Hamilton in his dark slacks, maroon tie, and white dress shirt, she couldn't envision how their time would be spent. The conversations during the long flight had been tense, because Hamilton was disappointed that the manhunt for Diego Guzman continued, and he was unable to field the call lines.

The pilot's voice came over the paging system, announcing a delay and new ETA in Honolulu. Meanwhile, a tall, broad-shouldered man in a suit strolled up the aisle, exchanged a few words with the flight attendant serving the first-class customers. He turned, headed back to economy seating, exchanging a look with Hamilton, then brushed his hip against the agent's shoulder.

Tessa noticed the rudeness. "What's that all about?"

Hamilton yawned. "Flight security. I bet he just checked to see if I was law enforcement."

She raised an eyebrow, then paused before asking another question.

"Agent Hamilton, since you're not supposed to be here, what FBI resources do you have to find Ray?"

"Don't worry about that. My ID will get us what we need. I have a fellow agent picking us up to take us to the local office in Honolulu. He owes me a couple of favors, thanks to me setting him up with his now-wife of two years."

She laughed.

"What's so funny?" He furrowed his brow.

"What makes you think a two-year marriage will get you favors?"

He chuckled. "He married my little sister."

Tessa returned a quirky smile. "Is she an agent, too?"

"Not FBI, actually a customs agent at the Port of Honolulu."

She swished her mouth to one side. *Will that be useful to locate Ray on a ship that is miles away – or not?*

"How long have you and Ray been married?"

"Less than two years. Why do you ask?"

"Just wondered how you were an expert on two-year-old marriages."

Tessa's face heated, and she turned to gaze out the window, trying to hide her embarrassment. The plane suddenly shook in the turbulent winds common above the Hawaiian Islands. Her body became rigid as chills ran through her.

Hamilton placed his large hand on Tessa's forearm and patted it. "We'll find Ray, don't you worry."

Still staring out the window at the now broken white fluffy clouds, the blue ocean came into sight, covered in an array of white spots appearing frozen upon its surface. How could she not worry? Worry about Ray, or worry more about working close with this strong, confident agent?

37

A white Ford Econoline Van sat idling, blocking the second lane of the concourse drive. No one in the driveway dared honk or make gestures, with the FBI emblem on the door. Special Agent Ted Augustine stood smoking nearby, wearing his dark blue, yellow-lettered FBI jacket. The nearby baggage handler waved his hand, trying to push the cigarette smoke away, frowning in response to the irritation. Agent Augustine smiled, dropped what remained of his Camel, and stomped it out on the concrete. Agent Hamilton and an attractive brunette exited the terminal through the sliding glass doors toting along small black bags.

"A little overdressed for Hawaii aren't you, Agent Hamilton?" The shorter agent reached out to shake hands.

"I had a little trouble at the office with call handling on the Guzman case."

"I get that. We heard about Guzman being sighted. Anderson would put all available agents on him." He reached his hand out toward Tessa. "You must be Mrs. Holland."

"You can call me Tessa, Agent..." she paused.

"Special Agent Ted Augustine, at your service. You can call me Agent Augustine in the office, Ted the rest of the time."

Hamilton pointed toward the Van. "You have the AC running in that thing? I'll need to dry clean this suit if I don't get out of this humidity soon."

"I'd apologize for the weather, but we at the FBI don't have a say in it. You're lucky. It's been raining for three days straight on account of a wet season storm." He turned, led them to the van, and opened the side sliding door.

"Do you want to stop at your hotel to change before we head to the office?" Augustine asked as they took seats next to each other in the rear double seat.

"No, let's get to your office, get updated on the *Arisha.*"

They arrived at the four-story beige brick building after a twenty-minute drive through the lush greens, still-wet roads and sidewalks. Tessa marveled at the scenery, nothing like she had ever seen before, at least in person. While they drove toward the security checkpoint, a roar came from the Kalaeloa Airport nearby as a gray P-3C Orion took off, leaving four black trails of exhaust from its roaring Allison T56-A-14 turboprop engines.

Tessa pointed. "Is that plane going to look for my husband?"

Augustine smiled, opening the glass swinging front door of the FBI check-in station. "I'm afraid that plane belongs to the US Navy. Not really at our disposal. We usually seek the US Coast Guard for our needs. They're much easier to work with."

After clearing security and moving the van inside the tall gate, they parked and walked toward the only visible entrance. Tessa had a guest pass with her photo on a bright lanyard, while Hamilton used his key card to open a door into a long, brightly lit hallway with carpet tile flooring. Pictures along the wall showed what appeared as earlier renditions of the FBI office, photos of the attack on Pearl Harbor, black and whites of some famous fugitives caught on the islands.

Augustine opened a door into a bright conference room, with an oval, dark-varnished wood table and wheeled fabric chairs. Two phones rested on the table, a cart with a glass water jug and coffee maker sat against the wall, and a small fridge on the floor. They sat, Tessa next to Hamilton, Augustine directly across.

"Do you have the number for the Honolulu Coast Guard?" Hamilton asked.

Augustine read the number from his cell phone. Hamilton dialed on the handset. After he introduced himself to the Coast Guard personnel who'd answered, they told him they would call back shortly.

"I understand we suspect *Arisha* of having Tessa's husband on board. What's your plan?" Augustine asked. "It's not like they're docked here, and they're outside our territorial waters from what little I know."

"I'm hoping the Coast Guard finds them and gets permission to board. If they let us, we might be allowed to go along."

"Unlikely, in my experience. Dangerous stuff boarding a ship at sea."

"Ray can't swim," Tessa interrupted.

Both agents furrowed their brows at the announcement.

"I mean, if it's dangerous to get Ray off a moving ship, if he falls in, he'll drown."

Hamilton and Augustine glanced at each other, apparently trying to articulate a response.

"Ray and I were on a Coast Guard helicopter once flying over the ocean. He told me when we came back how scared he was, even though we both had on life jackets." She glanced at her hands folded in her lap.

Hamilton asked, "Why were you on a Coast Guard helicopter over the ocean? When was this?"

Tessa looked up. "It's a long story. I shouldn't have even mentioned it. I think it's important to know Ray can't swim."

"Tessa, be assured, if Ray goes into the ocean, and I'm close by, I'll save him," Hamilton reassured her.

"Thank you. Is that something they teach at the academy?"

"No. My parents joined the YMCA when we were young."

"So did they teach you rescue techniques at the Y?"

He shook his head. "No."

"I think if Ray goes into the ocean, and I'm nearby, I'll save him."

"Tessa, I'm sure you're an excellent swimmer, but..."

She said quietly, "I was a lifeguard in high school and completed California State Parks Lifeguard Training Program in college. I'm certified in CPR, Public Safety First Aid, and open water search and rescue. Maybe best that I'll be rescuing my husband. You, Agent Hamilton, please make sure we don't get hurt by the bad guys."

"I'm impressed," Augustine interjected.

Hamilton stared at Tessa. "What about your hurt wing there?" He pointed at her wrapped right forearm.

"Bruised, remember?"

The phone rang. Agent Hamilton picked it up and pressed a speaker button so they all could hear the call. It was Commander Steven Chapman of the Honolulu base command. Agent Hamilton introduced all present.

"Agent Hamilton, my petty officer has been trying to reach you for hours, even left you a message on your office phone. We received a call back saying you were on your way here."

"We are here, Commander."

"Good, let me bring you up to speed on the *Arisha*. We sent an HC-130. They made contact, but the *Arisha* refused help. The HC-130 reports her listing, still disabled, now roughly forty-five miles north of Kauai, drifting southwest. We're sending a cutter to stand by. *Arisha* reported she will be back underway in the next couple of hours."

"Commander, you know she's suspected to be holding an American citizen, Ray Holland, captive."

"Yes, we have that information. Without permission from the ship's captain to board her, we have to wait on the State Department to give us a go ahead."

Hamilton groaned. "That could take days."

"All we can do is make them uncomfortable stationed nearby and wait."

"Can we get on that Coast Guard cutter?"

"I'm afraid not. She assisted in a rescue south of Pahala and is just now headed directly to *Arisha*'s last known. She's twelve hours away, just east of Hilo."

"If *Arisha* gets underway, we'll never catch her," Hamilton moaned.

"She'd quickly get out of our service area. We could request US Navy resources step in if the State Department authorizes it."

Tessa leaned forward and put a hand on her stomach. "We came all this way." A tear traced down her cheek, dripping onto the glossy table. She quickly wiped it away.

Hamilton turned, faced Tessa, and placed a hand gently on her shoulder. "What's the matter?" he whispered.

"Cramp." She waved him away. "It's nothing serious."

Hamilton picked up the handset. "Thank you, Commander,"

Before ending the call, he provided Chapman with his cell number, as well as Agent Augustine's.

"What now?" Tessa sniffled.

"We wait, go to the hotel to change, maybe get some dinner."

"Where are you staying?" Augustine asked.

"Embassy Suites Kapolei."

"Great, that's just down the street. I can get you a car from the motor pool."

"I'll order up a rental, thanks."

They stood up, Tessa slower. Hamilton asked, "You okay?"

"I think I'm just tired."

"Probably need something to eat. Like I said, we can go get something after we check in."

38

Upon arriving at the Embassy Suites Hotel, Agent Hamilton approached the reservation desk, checked in, and received two card keys. Tessa stood slightly behind and to the side, glanced around and sniffed the air. She tugged at his sleeve. "Smell that?"

"Smells like dinner," he said.

"Smells like I'm ready for a burger, fries and a Coke."

Overhearing the conversation, the young male host interjected, "That would be available in the Sprigs Grille, they're open till 9:00." He pointed to his left.

"Do you want to check into your room, freshen up?" Hamilton asked.

"No. I'm ready to eat."

Handing her the card key for her room, he said, "You go get dinner. I'm going to go to the room and change out of this suit."

"You want me to order you anything?"

"No, I'll look at the menu when I come back down."

Tessa shrugged and handed him her black bag.

"Can you toss that in my room?"

"Sure...but I need –"

Before he could finish, she was off in a dash toward the Sprigs Grille.

The young blond hostess smiled and glanced down, straightening her work blouse as Hamilton approached. "Dinner for one?"

"No, I'm with someone, brunette, with long hair."

Her smile softened as she took a single menu, turning toward the relatively empty seating area. "Right this way."

Seated in a booth, Tessa faced them as they approached. The hostess stopped and pointed to the table. "Is this your party?"

"Yes, thank you."

"Your server will be over in a moment." She strolled back toward her station.

Hamilton stood staring at Tessa, her half-eaten burger.

"You going to take a seat, Agent?"

"Could we switch? I usually face the entrance, personal preference."

She scooted over, slapped her hand on the seat a couple of times.

He slid in, bumping against her thigh, noticing her cola was in a tall clear glass and smelled of rum.

"Something to soften the ending of your day?"

"Yes, I'm afraid so. When they seated me and took my order, I had a bit of an emotional breakdown. Told the server more than I should. She brought me this, 'on the house.' I gave her a big tip, and she brought me two more."

"That's your third?"

She ducked her head.

"Well, you better down that burger, get more food in your stomach."

"What do you mean.?" She giggled. "This is my second."

"You've already eaten a full burger? Is this your second serving of fries?"

She nodded again. "They melt in my mouth."

"I can't imagine you eat like this all the time."

"Ray says I have a high metabolism."

The server approached and took Hamilton's order for prime rib and a whiskey with a beer chaser.

Tessa took another sip of her drink, then reached for her burger with both hands.

"Can I ask you a personal question?"

She bit into her burger and nodded.

"Do you and Ray not wear wedding rings?"

Tessa rolled her eyes, glanced at her left hand, and dabbed a napkin to her mouth as she chewed. After she swallowed, she said, "We do. They took mine off when they scanned me at the hospital. I thought about it. About putting it back on. It just seemed to upset me when I tried. Now it's hanging on a coffee cup holder in the cupboard. It reminds me I wanted to strangle him for causing our baby girl's death."

"He caused your baby's death?"

"No, I just keep remembering how mad I was. How reckless he is at times. I don't even think he realizes it."

"Why'd you marry him?"

"Wow, Agent Hamilton. Another very personal question."

"Sorry, I don't mean to pry. I just think a woman as beautiful as you could pick from numerous candidates."

"Do you really think I'm beautiful?" She grabbed his large, firm bicep, gave it a squeeze, and giggled.

The server approached with his tall beer and shot glass of dark whiskey. Hamilton lifted the liquid to his lips, tipped it back and swallowed. Shook his head, then chased it with the several gulps of beer.

Tessa looked in amazement. "Was it that good, Agent?"

"If you only knew."

Tessa lifted herself up and reached across the table for the Heinz Ketchup, sliding off Hamilton's thigh as she plunked back on the seat.

"Whoopsie, lost my balance." She slapped the bottle a couple times, dripping sauce on top of her golden fries, and looked up as the server approached with Hamilton's prime rib, baked potato, and shredded green beans.

As he dug in, she studied him. "You're quite the handsome hunk. Why is it you haven't found the love of your life?"

"I trust in fate to bring a woman into my life. But come on, being a federal agent, what woman could live with knowing her man could be killed any day on the job?"

"Don't be too hard on yourself. Lots of women could deal with that."

"Name one." He took a large bite of his prime rib.

Tessa cocked her head. "If I wasn't married to Ray, I could see being with a guy like you."

"Like me?"

"You know what I mean."

She played with her fries while watching Hamilton eat, occasionally licking ketchup off her fingers. Shortly after he finished, the server walked over.

"Anything else for you two? Dessert?"

"Maybe later." Hamilton requested the check. After paying, he pulled Tessa out of the booth gently, her long legs wobbly once on the floor. He placed his arm around her and guided her out of the restaurant, onto the elevator, then to her room. He pointed to the key card reader. Tessa reached into her back pocket, producing the key, and handed it to him. Once inside, he sat her down on a blue padded chair, gave the room a once-over, and drew back the sheets for her.

Tessa looked around the room. "Where's my bag?"

"It's in my room. Remember, you had your key?"

"Oh, makes sense."

"I'll go get it, be right back." Checking that he had both key cards, he left.

# # #

Tessa stood, walked gingerly into the bathroom, and glanced in the mirror.

"Ugh, who could call this beautiful?" She kicked the door shut. It didn't latch. Without giving it a second thought, she casually unfastened and took off her blouse and bra, slipped out of her flat shoes, and let her slacks fall to the ground. Socks and panties next, then she walked over, turned on the shower, and stepped inside once it was nice and hot, the way she liked it. She heard a knock at the door but ignored it as she relished the clean hot water and fragrant soap. She heard another sound but ignored it again. After stepping out of the shower she dried off. Then she stood naked in front of the mirror drying her hair with the hotel hair dryer, occasionally wiping the fogged-up mirror. Once her hair felt dry, she attempted to work it into a bun, but instead, wrapped it up in the damp towel and slipped the bathroom door open to go find her carry-on bag.

She gasped, not expecting to see someone in her room and in loungewear. Her mouth hung open, glaring at the man with hairless calves, a dragon-like tattoo on each leg. Her nightgown lay on the king size bed. The large man with damp hair glistening in the room light turned around, holding a large bottle.

"What are you doing in here?"

"You were in the shower when I brought your bag, so I showered and came to check on you. They brought us champagne."

Tessa stood frozen, her mind whirling. She simply stared at Hamilton, his shirt tight on his enormous arms, his knee-length shorts clung to every bulge of his lower torso. The room began to spin, then blackness.

39

The hotel room phone rang once. Tessa stirred, lying on her side, her head pounding as she faced the lone window in the suite. The room was brightening with the orange glow of daybreak. An unsettling suspicion arose, suggesting something was wrong. A musky smell, the taste of metal, but sweeter. She felt the silky sheets against her skin and heard a groan. She flipped onto her back, tilting her head, and there, beside her, was a familiar scalp. Large shoulders peaked out of the sheets.

"Oh my God," she gasped.

She scrambled from the comfort of the bed, met with the coolness of the air, confirmation of her nakedness. Desperately gazing around for something to put on, she found a towel on the floor and held it to her chest. Scrambling to her bag which lay on a luggage stand, she frantically dug through it until she found panties, bra, socks, shorts, and blouse. She sprinted into the bathroom, shut the door, and gazed into the mirror.

"What have I done, what have I done, what have I done?" she whispered. Grasping her towel and clothes to her bare chest, she fell to her knees, crying softly.

Moments passed. She finally moved and sat on the toilet. Still clinging to her towel and clothing, she rocked back and forth until she heard a noise. The door opened slowly. Hamilton stood there naked in the doorway. She took in every detail of the stunningly fit man standing before her. Turning her head, she covered her face with her hands full of clothes.

"Are you okay?" he asked. "I can explain, you know."

"There's no explaining this." She groaned as she threw her clothes to the floor, freeing her hands. She spread her legs, checked herself. Swollen, tender, slimy, she brought her hand to her face, paused. She convulsed. Quickly standing naked, she turned, lifted the toilet seat, and heaved what remained of her dinner. It burned her throat.

Hamilton stepped in, ran some water from the faucet into a fogged plastic glass, and handed it to her. Grabbing it, seeing him naked once more, she heaved again.

Running his large hand up and down her bare back, he said, "Tessa, I need you. Come on, you felt it. I love you."

Tessa heaved yet again, this time a dry gag. Hamilton reached around with his large hand, cupping her left breast, squeezing it gently. She placed her hand on his, trying to grip it hard enough for a reaction, but there was none. She pushed it away with her forearm.

"Tessa, you said you loved me last night, loved me holding you close."

Tessa held back another convulsion, reached up, and flushed away the bubbling waste. What had she done? She couldn't recall any of this. The words came out, "You took advantage of me. You raped me."

"Whoa, you consented to this. You said you loved me. I heard the words."

"I must've been drunk. I'm a married woman. I wouldn't have consented to this."

Hamilton stepped behind her, picked her up easily, turned her around, held her tight against his body, his breath hot in her face.

"Let's go back to bed. Forget about Ray. He's probably dead by now. You're a widow, time to move on, we're a perfect match, you said so."

Tessa could hardly breathe. He carried her into the bedroom and tossed her onto the messy bed. The phone rang again. With the brief distraction, she rolled off, scrambled to the bathroom, shut, and locked the door. *He must have set a wakeup call.* Jumping into the shower, and turning on the water, she scrubbed every inch of her body over and over to remove the shame she felt. Knowing Hamilton was still there, unpredictable – he could easily kick in the door – she hurried, dried off, and quickly dressed. Skipping applying makeup, she combed her hair, and pulled it back into a ponytail. A gentle knock came at the door.

"Leave, Agent Hamilton. You need to leave now."

"Tessa, I am so sorry. Maybe I got carried away. You said you love me. You sat close, gave me gentle nudges. What am I supposed to think?"

Tessa wondered how much she contributed to what had happened. So many emotions, too many. Her heart still ached at the loss of her baby, her mind still burned with uncontrolled rage toward Ray and his insensitivity. A man facing probable death. Then along came a strong, handsome, capable federal agent ready to help her rescue Ray. But now this.

"Agent Hamilton, you need to leave my room now."

"Okay, okay. I'll get dressed, go down, and bring up some breakfast. I'll set it outside your door, or we can eat together. It's entirely up to you." There was a pause, and the floor creaked as Hamilton moved around. Then the words, "Please forgive me."

Remaining silent, she waited until she heard the door open and shut. She peeked out the door to an empty room. Packing her carry-on luggage quickly, she was ready to go, to escape this situation, but what about Ray? She needed Agent Hamilton. Then she thought of Agent Augustine. Maybe he could help her instead. She sat at the dark oak veneer table, staring at the blank TV on the wall for several minutes. There'd be no more alcohol on this trip, but she needed something for her throbbing head.

A short time passed when a gentle knock came at the door.

"Who is it?"

"Breakfast," came Hamilton's familiar voice. A card key appeared from under the door. Tessa waited. She heard footsteps, followed by the sound of a door closing. When she opened the door, she saw a covered tray with a small white box labeled acetaminophen. A spark of joy filled her heart for a moment. At least he'd read her mind. Bringing the tray in, she set it on the dark oak table, and lifted the lid. A dish of scrambled eggs, two links of sausage, a tall glass of orange juice, and a white envelope sticking out from under the white porcelain dish.

Opening it, she pulled out a card. The front displayed a white cartoon image of a fat cat holding a red balloon with the word "Sorry" on it. Opening the card, the words, "Please forgive me," were sloppily written. *Who could write neatly with those large, powerful hands like his?* Although somehow it was elegantly signed, "Bryce Hamilton." Her mind raced at the possibilities. What if things were different now? This situation was as bad as it could possibly be.

When was the last time Ray said he was sorry? In the hospital? *I sent him on his way. His way to being kidnapped, maybe tortured and possibly dead now.* Putting her hand to her stomach, she bent double in reaction to another cramp. Maybe she should go to the hospital, see if something was wrong. But she wasn't sure she could be truthful, not knowing for sure what had taken place overnight. Certainly, sex with a single man, not her husband. A man not versed in being gentle, perhaps. Her first sex in months due to her pregnancy. The cramp passed. She sat up straight, raised the glass of orange juice, and took a sip.

It tasted good. She took another sip, then a bite of the eggs, and kept at it until her plate was clean. She heard what sounded like a door shutting in the hallway and footsteps that stopped in front of her door. A piece of paper appeared under the door; her key card still rested next to it. Picking them both up, she put the card on the table, and opened the folded paper. It read, "Headed to the field office to check on the *Arisha*. Will be back soon, Bryce."

40

Ray lay on his back, his eyes fluttering open as a throbbing pain pulsed through his forehead. Recognizing the pale paint of his quarters, he understood his situation hadn't changed. The room still rolled gently with the sea, no noise but the distant diesel generator rumbling. His internal clock told him it had been over four hours, and they still weren't underway.

As he attempted to sit up, his arm made contact with warm skin, prompting him to turn and gaze. His body tensed. Angelina lay next to him, hair tied up in a messy bun. Wearing an extra-large blue and white horizontally striped t-shirt, she lay facing away. The T-shirt had drifted up, exposing her hip and buttocks. He reached over and gently shook her.

"Angelina, wake up."

She stirred and sighed. Turning and seeing Ray, she smiled.

Ray frowned. "What are you doing here still? If Vlad, or anyone else comes, this would be bad for both of us."

"I locked the door. No one comes."

"Angelina. They could still come."

"You don't understand. Vlad, he only wants one thing at a time. Ship must be fixed, that is his one thing. When ship starts, then maybe he will come find me for sex or something. You, he knows you are stuck here. He will come, but only after sex, or maybe he won't need sex. I don't know. I will get dressed and go find him. See what he wants."

She rolled over on top of him and stopped. The gaping T-shirt granted Ray a clear sight of nothing underneath. She brought her head down, kissed his forehead, then rolled off the bed. Raising the T-shirt over her head, she dropped it to the floor, picked up her dirty panties, short skirt, and blouse, and put them on.

"I will go find Vlad. He sees me, he won't want sex... I know. I will go change, get you some food, okay?"

Ray lay there wondering why this young woman would take these chances with a man that clearly abused her physically and emotionally. Naive she might be, but she was clearly dancing on dangerous ground with this unstable Russian man. His life, unfortunately, was in the hands of the former spy, Dimitri Mishkin, and his vengeful son.

His device could save Tessa from joining him in this dilemma. How much danger was Tessa really in? What did Vladislav have in resources to get to her? What of the FBI or local police? He was kidnapped. Where were they now? Were they protecting Tessa? There was no way to know inside a disabled ship wavering in the ocean. He needed a solution.

He glanced over at his GG device on the floor, along with most everything else not secured due to the rocking of the ship. He lay thinking: the magnetic orientation of the stones had clearly been a factor in the directional force of the GG device. Successful in the test in the desert, which dug a hole vertical in the desert floor, he was confident he could eliminate the directional force all together and provide a more neutral result, creating a static level of levitation. Manipulating the orientation of the stones in the array could provide the neutral result. If so, the small donut-shaped device may provide an escape opportunity.

He still needed to dial down the power output from what had just rotated and held the sixty-thousand-ton ship in place. Reducing the quantity of stones with fewer layers in the array might work. He could use the other small housing and components to save time, but they were still stored somewhere on the ship. He needed Angelina's help.

41

Angelina placed her hand on the passageway wall as she made her way to Vlad's quarters, compensating for the continued rolling of *Arisha* at the mercy of the current sea state. She pushed open the door to the quarters. Vlad lay on his back on his small bed, his eyes closed. He was dressed in clean black pants and white t-shirt, his left forearm wrapped. She stepped over to him and placed her hand gently on his shoulder; he remained motionless. Scanning the room, she noticed an open bottle of Vodka on the small wooden table, an empty clear glass next to it. She stepped over to the table, poured the glass half full, and took a sip, sitting down in one of the wooden chairs. She raised the glass, took another sip and coughed.

Vladislav opened his eyes, turned his head, furrowed his brow. "Where have you been sleeping? I come here and you are not here." His voice was calm.

"How would you know I am not here?" She scowled.

He rolled onto his side and sat up, crouched over. "I come here expecting to find you for sex, and talk."

"I do not know your schedule. Remember we have Mr. Holland to care for. Leonid is too busy and doesn't know English." She poured more Vodka. The bottle tapped against the glass brim.

Vladislav stood, placed a hand on the wall, and cringed at the pain in his bruised leg. "You did not answer my question," he growled.

"Which question?"

"Where you sleep?" he screamed.

"Easy Vlad. I sleep here. I sleep where I can."

His eyes opened wide. "You sleep with Holland?"

For a moment, Angelina sat frozen in the chair, then lifted the clear glass to her lips, the translucent contents shaking. She took a sip. "I come looking for you to sleep with, you are not here. Why would I sleep with Holland?"

"You smell of Holland."

"What would you know of Holland's smell. You spend no time with him."

Vladislav stepped over, leaned down, placed his face to Angelina's neck, took a deep breath. "He has touched you."

"No."

"Then you have touched him."

"No."

He stood, grabbed the clear glass out of her hand and poured the contents in his mouth, then backhanded her face with the hand grasping the glass. A glistening of fragments flew across the room. Angelina collapsed across the table. Her hand on her face, she groaned, looking back toward Vladislav.

"I do not trust you." He walked over to a black nylon bag on the floor by the bed. He pulled out a dark slender object and palmed it in his hand. "You are soiled goods, you should look it."

He pressed a button, and a shiny silver blade popped out. Angelina sat up quickly and pushed the chair back with her legs. It fell to the floor.

He swung the blade toward her face, and she threw up her arm, blocking his forearm. She cringed at the sharp sting and grabbed her arm. Vladislav swung again toward her face. She ducked, a near miss, so she thought. But when she stood, a warm liquid ran down the side of her face, onto her neck. She cast her eyes downward, catching sight of a chunk of flesh, its vibrant red hue splattered across the floor. Reaching up to the side of her head, she found wetness and the top of her ear missing.

She glared at Vladislav and ground her teeth as she saw his arm coming around for another strike. She lifted her leg and slammed a square kick into his chest. He fell back to the floor. An astonished look on his face, he scrambled to get up. Angelina sprinted toward him, and drew up her leg again, planting it square in his groin. He screamed and pulled up his legs to his chest. She dashed to the first of the cabinets in the room, opening it. Not finding what she wanted, she moved to the next. When she opened the third cabinet, she pulled out the small red plastic container labeled "First Aid."

She glanced back at Vladislav as he was now on his hands and knees preparing to get up. Running to his side, she placed another kick, this time square in the middle of his back. He screamed as he collapsed flat on the floor. She paused, wiped her hand across her wet face, licked the blood from her hand and spat it toward his head. He moved slowly, groaning.

"Angelina, enough," he hollered.

She wasn't done. Standing over him she watched as drops of her blood collected on his shirt. Her face warmed with wrath as he raised up again. She took a step back and launched a robust kick square onto his ass. He launched forward and crumpled to the floor.

Angelina opened a dresser drawer, palmed some clean clothes and bolted out the door.

42

A knock came at the door. Ray turned, lifted his pen from his notepad that held an array of calculations. The door slowly opened. Angelina stood, now in tight blue jeans and a loose-fitting light blue T-shirt, holding a tray in both hands. He inhaled the fragrance of cooked beef, garlic, potatoes, and the familiar, "Happy" by Clinique perfume of Tessa's. Angelina wasn't smiling. Her face had more of a stern, determined look. Then he noticed a dark circle under her left eye. Worse yet, her left ear was streaked with dark red, more visible between the strands of her blond hair. A sloppily applied bandage held her hair away from her head.

Not able to stand, Ray asked, "My God, what happened to you?"

Angelina set the tray down. As he slid his notes to the side, she studied the work, the numbers, the small illustrations.

"I went to see Vlad. It was a bad time."

"Did he hit you?"

"More, he cut me. Lucky, I moved. He wanted to scar me so no man would ever love me."

"Why would he –?"

Angelina interrupted, "Someone in crew told him I was with you, maybe too much. Vlad is...*revnivyy*, jealous, I think is your American word."

"Bastard," Ray growled.

"What is bastard?"

"An evil man. A terrible man to hurt such a beautiful woman."

"I'm afraid I am not beautiful now." She pulled her hair back on the left side, pulled off the loosely wrapped bandage, revealing the top half of her ear missing. A mix of red and clear fluids slowly dripped.

Ray gasped.

"You see. This is his *mstit'* – punishment for looking at another man. Now scared I am ugly. No man will have me."

"That's it. I won't help this man...this monster," Ray growled.

Angelina leaned toward him, placing both hands on his shoulders, almost sitting on his tray of food.

"No, you must complete this work. He will kill you, surely. He only needs one reason to kill anyone on this ship. He is so angry." A tear trickled from her bruised eye. "He is only happy the ship's engine will start soon. We head to Russia."

Ray gazed at Angelina, wondering what he could do. His throat clinched tight. How now to protect her? Still keep Vladislav from going after Tessa, maybe save his own life. If that was possible? So far, his calculations proved it doable if he was careful.

"Angelina. I need the remaining components of what Vlad took from my home. Can you take me to them?"

Angelina glanced at his scribbled notes, still holding his shoulders. "You have plan."

"Yes, I think it will work."

"I know your work, very powerful. I know levitation, you said. So, your plan, can you levitate off Arisha?"

"Yes, I believe we can if I can get the rest of what I need."

"You said we." Still smiling, she squeezed his shoulders. "We. You will levitate me also?"

"Yes, it's possible."

She leaned close, kissed his forehead, kissed his nose. Gazing into his shocked blue eyes, she hesitated, then placed her lips on his. After pulling away briefly, she opened her eyes and leaned in once more, pressing her lips against his in another passionate kiss. As she gradually pulled back, Ray's eyes widened, his mouth still agape in astonishment.

"Sorry." She stood, releasing her grip.

"It's okay." He smiled and leaned forward in an attempt to stand; Angelina pulled him up. He hopped to the cupboard, opened it, and pulled out a first aid kit. Shuffling the items around, he found a tube of antiseptic and a cloth wrap, then he pointed to the chair he'd been seated in. Angelina sat. After drying the seeping fluids on her ear, he applied antiseptic, then wrapped and taped it. She thanked him and told him they should go now to the storeroom, leaving his cooling meal on the table.

After taking several minutes to hop continuously, stopping to navigate through narrow doorways, they made it to the storeroom. Ray scanned his scattering of components and soon recognized everything he needed. He collected more of the fluorescent fusion stones, dropping them into an empty paint can. He bent and broke off some of the meshed array trays which held the fusion stones in place inside the large GG unit. After acquiring a pair of tin snips from the tool room, they successfully returned to his quarters. He was ready to sit, exhausted from all the hobbling. Angelina was out of breath, having assisted Ray in walking and carrying multiple components. Beads of sweat rolled down her face, her T-shirt sticking to her skin. Ray sat down hard, glancing at his cold meal, still waiting to be eaten.

"I can warm that for you," she offered.

"No, I can." He pointed to the small microwave oven on the counter.

Angelina, still breathed hard. "I need to go now before anyone tells Vlad I'm here. I will hide from him. He cannot hit me. Leonid will help me. He does not like Vlad."

"What if I need something?"

"I will send Leonid. He only knows Russian, so write what you need. He will give to me."

"Batteries, I will need more D batteries."

Angelina smiled. "I will find." Stepping next to Ray, she hugged his head, holding it against her soft damp T-shirt.

"I know you are smart. You will save Angelina." She paused, still holding his head against her soft bosom.

She slowly released her grip. Ray looked up at her. "How much do you weigh?"

"You don't know? You guess?"

"Actually, I forgot. It's important."

Angelina raised an eyebrow, placed a finger to her temple.

"Kilograms or pounds?"

"Pounds please."

"Oh, one twenty, maybe one twenty-five," She pinched her waist. Ray wrote it down. Angelina then turned and walked out. Just as she was about to leave, she turned back, blew a sweet kiss, and gently closed the door.

# # #

A thunder-like roar rattled the *Arisha* as she continued to rock gently in a calm sea, broken gray clouds moving quickly overhead. Cheers could be heard in the hallways, as one engine had been restarted. Captain Konstantin Semenov spread his legs slightly as he stood, his hands on the wheel of the *Arisha*, turning to starboard now that the ship was in motion again. Just in time, as a US Coast Guard cutter approached.

"Remind me to give Sergei a bottle of scotch for his fine work." Vladislav sat on a cushion on a steel bench near the rear of the bridge.

"Your celebration may be too soon." Captain Semenov pointed to the white ship in the distance.

"They can't do anything but bother us." He slowly stood, taking in the improving skies and sea.

"We'll be lucky to do fifteen knots on one engine."

Vladislav raised the large binoculars from the counter, looked through them in the direction of the cutter. "It will be enough. We are underway. They will grow tired and turn back."

"They may know of your guest, you forget. Contact their State Department seeking permission to board us."

"If they try, our guest will go for a swim after I shoot him."

Semenov ran his hand across his beard. "They will still board us."

"They won't find anything. You assured me our papers are in order. Crew is good."

"We have another problem, I'm afraid."

"What is that?"

Captain Semenov pointed at a sheet of paper next to the radar. "The latest weather forecast. There is another storm between us and Vladivostok. We must alter course, either toward Japan, or a slow northerly direction and wait for it to pass."

"This would be why *Afina* won't come. My father sent me a message. *Afina* was forced to turn back, not able to assist us."

"You should let your father know of our further delay, and the American ships. Maybe he has some advice."

Vladislav walked over to the bench and sat, shifting his body and winced.

Semenov stared and pointed at the cushion. "Are you injured?"

He grabbed the cushion. "You mean this?

"You move like you're in pain."

"I am. Angelina took her frustrations out on me."

Semenov lifted his captain's hat, ran his hand across his head. "I doubt that is all that took place. What have you done?"

"Nothing. Nothing she didn't ask for."

Placing his hat firmly on his head. "That troubles me. Where is she? What are her injuries?"

Vladislav stood, placed a hand on the wall to steady his balance. "I will find her. She is probably with Holland."

"What..are..her..injuries?" he snapped.

"She is not dead or dying."

Semenov stepped in front of Vladislav, blocking his path to the door. "Vlad, I grow tired of your avoidance of what I ask. I am captain. Tell me, what are her injuries."

"I cut her. She'll be fine."

Leaning over and grabbing the cushion, Semenov handed it to him. "I will send Leonid to check on your Angelina. I don't trust you to care for her. You should be grateful. I may be saving you from further injury."

Semenov stood rigid as Vladislav stepped around him and exited the bridge.

43

Hamilton sat at the conference room table, contemplating what had transpired in the last twelve hours. He took a sip from a paper cup of black coffee as he waited for Agent Augustine's arrival with an update on the *Arisha*. The sun was bright, a clear blue sky visible through the tinted windows enhanced the deep blue water of Oneula Beach.

The door opened. Augustine, dressed in a dark coat, maroon tie, and slacks, entered carrying two white paper cups in his hands. "You have coffee already?"

"I got an early start." Hamilton reached up to take the spare cup.

"Long night? Is Mrs. Holland still pretty upset about Ray and our lack of progress?"

"She's upset, that's apparent." Hamilton swirled the last of his colder cup, tipped it up, swallowed its contents.

Augustine raised an eyebrow and sat down across from him. Pulling a piece of paper from his inside jacket pocket, he placed it on the table in front of Hamilton.

"There's not much for good news coming from the Coast Guard. The *Arisha* is underway again, but slowly. Probably running on one engine, or reduced power, or both. She has a bigger problem. There is a deep low-pressure system stalled north of her position. This is actually to our benefit. The Coast Guard cutter *Rush* is on the scene now, shadowing her movements. The State Department is dealing with two Americans under arrest and suspected of spying, being held in Moscow. The *Arisha* situation is off their radar."

"We need to get out there."

"Not without the Coast Guard."

"You were in the Navy, a Seal Team member, right?"

Augustine rolled his eyes. "That was a long time ago."

"You know how to board a ship at sea."

"Hamilton, I don't know what you're thinking, or who you're trying to impress. Without proper resources and authorization, boarding a Russian merchant vessel underway is not happening."

"Then Mr. Holland is a dead man, and Mrs. Holland is a soon-to-be widow."

"I'm sorry, we don't have —" The phone on the table beeped, and a voice interrupted, "A call for Agent Hamilton."

"Take a message please," Augustine said.

"Wait, that might be Tessa." Hamilton reached for the phone.

"Or Special Agent Johnson wanting to know why you haven't checked in."

Agent Augustine picked up the phone, called the reception desk. "Who was the call from, Cindy?"

Agent Augustine stared at Hamilton as he listened and hung up. "It was Tessa. Said to tell you she was going to the hospital. Something about bleeding."

"Oh, shit." Heat rose up Hamilton's neck.

"Oh, shit is right. Why is she bleeding?"

Hamilton looked at his coffee cup in his hand, didn't respond.

"Where is she bleeding?"

Hamilton remained silent.

Augustine leaned forward. "You didn't."

"I'm afraid we did."

"Consensual?"

"I thought so."

Augustine stood, his chair slapping against the wall. "This could get ugly for you, end your career with the Bureau."

Hamilton buried his face into his hands. "I know. Been thinking about it all morning."

"Any conclusions?"

"One."

Augustine turned and gazed out the window. "Which is?"

"Save Mr. Holland."

"Like I said before, we don't have the authority or resources yet."

Hamilton slapped his hand on the table and stood. "I'll do it alone then."

"I can't let you do that."

He crushed the coffee cup in his hand and tossed it to the floor. "You can't stop me. You have no authority over me here."

"It's suicide. They're fifty miles offshore, sailing at fifteen knots in two-to-six-foot seas."

"Hey, pirates in the Gulf of Aden off Somalia can do it with no real training."

"They have support ships nearby."

Hamilton stepped over to Augustine and tugged on his jacket. "Sounds like I have the Coast Guard nearby if I get in trouble."

"If they see you come in on the radar, they'll stop you for sure."

"I have to try. My career is likely ending here, so maybe I can redeem some worthiness, or at least forgiveness from Tessa."

Augustine tugged his arm free from Hamilton's grip, furrowed his brow. "I still won't let you go. I'll cuff you to this table if I have to."

"All right, all right. I'll go see Tessa at the hospital, update her on no good news."

"I'll come with you."

"No. Best if I do this alone. We have lots to go over."

"Okay, call me. Let me know how she's doing."

44

Hamilton opened the trunk of his Ford T-bird rental in the FBI lot and tossed his jacket in, as well as his shoulder holster and two Glock 23's. He hopped in and drove toward the Honolulu marina.

Once at the marina, he knew what he was looking for, so he scanned the docks until he found a group of high-speed inflatable boats, similar to those used by Navy Seals. Noticing a sign for "Pick Marine and Charter," he scanned the offices that ran along the boulevard until he spotted "Pick." The window was covered in ads for boats for sale from catamarans, to mono hull sailboats to large fifty-foot power boats.

Pulling open the glass door, he was greeted by a bell chime and a young blonde wearing a red halter top, white shorts and too much eyeliner. He pulled out his credentials, holding them out. She stood to read it carefully and made a note. "What can we do for you, FBI Agent Hamilton?"

"I need to rent one of your high-speed inflatables."

"Sure, we can help you with that. They're only available captained and are two hundred dollars an hour."

"I won't need a captain."

"I'm afraid that's the only way we can do this. Insurance reasons, you understand."

"Is the owner here? May I speak with him?"

"One moment." She frowned as she pressed a button on her phone. "I have an FBI Agent here that wants to rent an HSI without a captain." There was a pause as she listened, the answered, "Okay, thanks." She hung up, turned her attention back to Hamilton. "He'll be right out."

Hamilton stood and waited as a nicely dressed, short man in bleached white pants, thin nylon teal button-down shirt, came from the back. He looked up at Hamilton. "You must be FBI."

"Special Agent Hamilton." He held out his credentials again.

"Nice to meet you. I'm James Pick." He reached up to shake hands. His hand disappeared inside Hamilton's. "I understand you want to rent one of our high-speed inflatables."

"That's correct."

"Pardon me for asking, but doesn't the FBI have their own high-speed boats?"

"They don't here in Hawaii."

"For insurance reasons, I'm afraid we have to captain the boat. Is that okay, Agent Hamilton?"

"I'm afraid not."

"Then all I can say is, sorry."

"Do you have any for sale, then?"

"Now, that I can do." James smiled and turned to the young woman. "Tracy, we'll be on B dock." He grabbed a wireless radio from the counter.

They trotted down to the dock. The wind picked up as the sun continued to rise in the clearing blue sky. A scattering of flags full of ads on the docks fluttered in the breeze. Hamilton and Pick were soon standing in front of a thirty-two-foot inflatable with fake teak accents, ample seating, and a table. Powered by twin black three hundred horsepower Mercury outboard motors, it featured a center mounted steering console.

Hamilton shook his head. "No." Pointing down the dock to a smaller, more familiar boat, a twenty-two-foot Zodiac Hurricane. It also came with the center steering console, although it contained a two-hundred-thirty horsepower inboard out-drive engine, and radar mounted on a radar frame. Hamilton knew this would do the job. He just needed to somehow take possession of it. "How much?"

"We used to use this one for whale tours, but —"

Hamilton interrupted, "How much?"

"Eighty-five thousand cash price."

"Terms?"

"We can do zero percent, probably ten years. If you have good credit, maybe two thousand down."

"Let's do it."

Pick reached out to congratulate Hamilton, who had already headed back toward the office. An hour later Hamilton had the keys, temporary title paperwork, inflatable personal flotation device, full set of foul weather gear, a gaff hook, and 75 feet of rope. Familiar with the workings of a boat when he was a teen living on Lake Michigan, he was confident he could get off the dock soon and be on his way to the *Arisha*. At a 30-knot capable speed, he felt he could reach the ship before dark.

45

Agent Augustine arrived at Kapiolani Medical Center, and at the information desk he confirmed Tessa Holland was being cared for. Augustine showed his credentials to the security guard and the triage staff, then they led him to a private room where Tessa lay on a gurney in a blue gown. Her eyes lit up at the sight of Augustine.

"Where's Agent Hamilton?" Augustine asked.

"I haven't seen him."

He glanced at the closed clear glass door, then asked, "How are you doing?"

"The doctor said I'll live."

"That's good." He stood, unsettled, shuffling.

Tessa frowned. "What is it?"

"I thought Hamilton would be here. He should be here. He should be concerned about your wellbeing."

Tessa gazed down to her hands resting on her belly, quiet.

"I think I know more than I should," Augustine admitted.

"The taking advantage of an unconscious woman, or the rape part?"

There was a long pause, Augustine fidgeting and shuffling his feet more. "His career in the Bureau is over, you know."

She shrugged. "I guess it would be if I file a police report."

"You tell the doctor?"

"Hard to hide the damage. I explained the recent accident, aborted fetus, and lack of sex. I didn't name names. For all he knew, my husband wasn't gentle."

"What are you going to do?"

"I really don't know. I'm mad at Hamilton for what he did, could be pregnant with his baby for all I know."

"Oh shit." Heat rose up Augustine's neck and he turned to hide his face. "Are they going to admit you?"

"No, just waiting on blood test results. They already did an ultrasound, and everything is where it's supposed to be."

"Could you excuse me a moment?" Augustine stepped outside the patient room, pulled out his cell phone, and dialed. He paced the hallway for several moments waiting for an answer from the hotel clerk. A few minutes later, he stepped back into Tessa's room.

"Hamilton checked out of his room. He still has his rental though."

"Where did he go?"

"I can think of only two places. The airport or the marina."

Tessa's face held a puzzled look. "Why would he go to the marina?"

"He wants to save your husband, or at least that's what he said. Owes it to you. He wanted me to help him. I refused, tried to talk sense into him. What he wants to do is dangerous and will probably get him killed. I threatened to cuff him to the office table to stop him. Then he seemed to have a change of heart and said he was coming here. I better head down the marina and try to find him."

"Wait, I'm coming with you."

"You can't, can you?"

"Draw that curtain, step outside, and guard the door. I'm getting dressed."

A few minutes passed, Tessa slid open the glass door, hopping as she slid on her left shoe. Her doctor stepped into the hallway from a room two doors down.

She shouted, "Sorry. I gotta go."

Agent Augustine shrugged his shoulders, smiled, and grabbed Tessa by the forearm, leading her toward the exit. The doctor shook his head, scribbled some notes on a clipboard in his hand, then walked across the hall into the next room.

Taking about thirty minutes to arrive at the Marina due to traffic, the FBI-emblemed van wasn't easy to weave through busy streets and intersections. Knowing Hamilton's rental was a mocha brown Ford T-bird, they drove around scanning the parking lot. Ten minutes later they spotted it.

"He probably chartered a boat," Augustine said. "A fast boat. Probably a high-speed inflatable like we used in the Navy."

He saw a few RIB inflatables scattered across a couple of docks. Along the boulevard, he spotted various charter companies, intermingled with marine supply companies and restaurants. He began at one end and approached each charter company, inquiring if Hamilton had visited them. After about twenty minutes, they found Pick's. A young blonde woman greeted them at the desk and confirmed Hamilton had been there and purchased a boat. After getting the boat size and type, Augustine rushed out to see if he was still on the dock or fueling at one of the fuel docks nearby.

"Wait." He ran back into Pick's, asking the young woman if they could borrow the VHF radio and try to reach Hamilton. She obliged, handing him one of their portable units. Augustine, using his name, tried calling Hamilton on Channel 16. The young woman provided Augustine with the boat registration number, which he tried to hail as well, but he received no response.

Next he hailed the Coast Guard, and they responded immediately. The Coast Guard requested Agent Augustine switch to channel 22 to continue the conversation. Augustine provided limited information about Hamilton, mentioning only that he was an FBI Agent, missing, and had departed Honolulu less than an hour earlier.

The Coast Guard told Augustine to stand by. Then they heard the announcement come across the wall mounted VHF next to the young woman, which monitored channel 16.

"All stations, all stations, all stations. This is the United States Coast Guard, Sector Honolulu. We have received a report of a missing boater in the vicinity of Pearl Harbor. Reported to be operating a twenty-two-foot Zodiac Hurricane. A single operator described as male wearing a red life jacket and black pants. If you have any information regarding this boater's whereabouts, please contact the United States Coast Guard immediately on Channel 16. This is the United States Coast Guard, Honolulu, out."

After the Coast Guard called Augustine back on the VHF radio, they exchanged phone numbers for updates. He thanked the young woman for her help and handed back the portable VHF. Then they stepped outside into the building winds.

"What now?" Tessa asked.

"Let's head down to the Coast Guard. See what we can shake loose."

46

A soft knock sounded on Ray's door, then it gradually swung open. A bald man stood in the opening, dressed in a horizontal striped knit shirt and dark pants. He stepped into his quarters and said something in Russian. A lean man, his hairless arms were scraped up, probably thanks to the ship's hard turn and literal bounce. A simple band-aid rested on his chin.

Ray asked, "Leonid?"

"Da." He nodded.

Ray was relieved they could at least communicate on a basic level, at least with a head gesture. He handed Leonid a note on a half sheet of paper, showing the need for eight D batteries, more copper wire, and solder. He also added a request for the most recent global position, heading, and speed. Doubtful he would get that information, he wanted a backup plan for taking control of the ship's movements using his GG device if it came to a Plan B. Leonid took the list and glanced at it. Then he shrugged his shoulders, waved awkwardly, and stepped out the door, closing it.

Twenty minutes passed, and another knock came at his door. It was Leonid again, his dark eyebrows raised, a wrinkled forehead, the note still crumpled in his hand. He spoke in a defiant panicked tone, but Ray couldn't discern a single Russian word other than "Angelina" mentioned several times. Something was clearly wrong. *What has Vladislav done now? Killed Angelina, maimed her again?* Leonid stopped talking, held his hand up, and ran out the door.

Not in any condition to follow, Ray lowered himself to the floor, crawled to the doorway, and looked down the passageway in each direction. Hearing footsteps in the distance, he knew someone was nearby. Then he recognized the skinny Leonid briskly striding toward him, another man close behind. When he reached Ray, he helped pick him up, and sat him back in the chair at his table. The other man with black-as-night hair and dark brown eyes spoke.

"I am Mikaela, I can translate for Leonid."

Leonid rattled off a paragraph of information in Russian to Mikaela, who turned toward Ray.

"Leonid cannot find Angelina. She is not in her quarters, or with Vlad. No one has seen her. Leonid fears she is dead or hiding on board."

Ray, clearly amazed with his English, asked, "Does Leonid know Vlad cut Angelina and beat her?"

Mikaela translated the question to Leonid, who nodded.

Ray thought a moment, then asked, "Would it be possible to remove Vlad's control over me being a prisoner on this ship, put him in a brig or something?"

Mikaela paused, said a few words to Leonid, then said, "Vlad is the only person on board armed with guns. His father owns and runs this ship. We all work for him. If we go against Vlad, we risk being shot, thrown overboard, or lose our jobs." After exchanging several sentences with Leonid, Mikaela turned to face Ray.

"There will be no mutiny on this ship. We respect our captain completely, only Vlad is troublesome. No crew will stand up to Vlad except Angelina. We must find Angelina."

"I understand." Ray wondered if these men knew of his fate. He had nothing to lose fighting Vlad or killing Vlad, although he wasn't a killer, never having even fired a gun before. All he had was his wits. To outsmart Vlad, he needed Angelina, or someone else in the crew, to help him.

Mikaela said, "We must go to find Angelina."

Ray pointed to the list in Leonid's hand. "Can Leonid get the items on the list?"

Mikaela reached out. Leonid handed him the list. He scanned it and read it off to Leonid who said, "Yes," followed by several indiscernible words understood by Mikaela.

"Leonid will get you these items soon."

Ray thanked them both. Leonid nodded, shook the list in his hand, and smiled. Then the men walked out the doorway, closing it behind them. Ray buried his head in his hands. If Angelina was dead, his life was over. There would be no escape without her. He leaned forward, grimaced, and held his stomach, then heaved a dry convulsion. He grimaced once more as his head throbbed.

What was happening to him? Did he have feelings for Angelina, now possibly dead? His anger rose like lava at such a vicious man to hurt such a kind, beautiful woman. This man deserved to die, just like his brother Viktor. He'd cut Angelina's ear practically off. Vlad must die at the hands of a GG device, just as his brother had, the *Arisha* at the bottom of the ocean as its fate. He had everything he needed to sink her. Maybe the Coast Guard was close by to save those of the crew that could swim and make it to lifeboats.

He was not able to swim, or walk, so his life was over. He was confident Tessa would eventually move on, the strong woman she was. Maybe she regretted those things said in anger. This wasn't her fault. She should move onto a happier life.

47

Trailing a faint cloud of diesel exhaust smoke, the dark ship's contrast was easy to spot against the hazy blue horizon. The US Coast Guard cutter *Rush*, commanded by CO Anthony Barstow, quickly gained on the slow-moving merchant vessel. Barstow held the large binoculars to his eyes, his cap turned backward as he studied the vessel.

His latest message from the Honolulu command: - a disabled Russian Merchant ship, with a possible American citizen on board, held against his will. Now slowly underway, there had been no word from the US State Department regarding authorization to board her.

"Let's approach her from our starboard, get a good look at her," Barstow ordered his helmsman, standing outside the doorway of the bridge. "Maybe she will hail us first."

As the Coast Guard clipper *Rush* approached the *Arisha*, neither Barstow, nor his OOD (officer of the deck), noticed any on-deck activity. They stepped back inside the less windy bridge and readied to hail her.

"*Arisha, Arisha, Arisha*, this is US Coast Guard Vessel *Rush*, do you read?"

"US Coast Guard *Rush*, this is *Arisha*. We read you," a voice called from the speaker on the bridge.

"*Arisha*, switch to channel 22," Barstow ordered.

"Roger, switching to 22," the voice responded.

"*Arisha*, are you in need of assistance?"

"No assistance is needed, US Coast Guard."

"*Arisha*, this is Commanding Officer Barstow. May I speak with your captain?"

The radio was silent for a long moment, then a voice responded, "This is Captain Semenov of *Arisha*."

"Captain, this is Commanding Officer Barstow of the *Rush*. We have received a message from our command that you may have an American citizen on board. Is this true?"

The radio was silent for another long moment. Barstow looked at his OOD. "That wasn't supposed to be a hard question for a captain of a ship."

"Commander, I only have Russian crew on my ship," Semenov finally responded.

"Captain, since your last port of call was San Francisco, I request permission to board your vessel and conduct an inspection."

"Commander, that won't be needed. Our papers are in order. We cleared your US port with no issues."

A page came over the bridge intercom: "Bridge, small vessel incoming at high speed. Won't answer to a hail. Distance two miles, heading three-two-seven degrees, thirty knots, no identification, appears to be a small RIB."

"Radio *Arisha* to stand by on channel 22." Barstow ordered, as he looked at his officer who handed him the large binoculars. "Call general quarters."

The officer of the deck pressed a button on the bridge console, picked up a microphone, and announced general quarters. An alarm sounded in the bridge and throughout the ship as the crew scrambled to their pre-assigned stations, donning their appropriate gear.

Commander Barstow grabbed the microphone. "All hands, this is Commander Barstow. Change course to one-seven-zero degrees, full ahead."

A response came back, acknowledging the change. Two other officers on the bridge scanned the darkening horizon for the incoming vessel, as did Commander Barstow. Another call came into the bridge from the CIC: "Bridge, vessel heading three-three-zero degrees, thirty knots. It's on an intercept with the *Arisha*."

"Keep trying to hail them," Barstow ordered.

"Aye aye, sir, we will continue to hail," the response came back.

"Contact bearing three-two-zero degrees", the officer of the deck called out.

"I see it." The commander picked up the radio, making another announcement, "All hands, this is Commander Barstow, change course to two-zero-zero degrees, maintain full ahead."

"Aye aye, sir, course two-zero-zero degrees, maintain full ahead."

Suddenly an announcement came over the radio, and a new alarm sounded. "Man overboard, man overboard."

Commander Barstow picked up the radio. "All hands, all hands, man overboard, man overboard. Helm come about, coarse zero-three-zero degrees, ahead slow. Deploy a rescue boat."

Barstow set the microphone down. "Eyes in the water for our crewman."

Three officers on the bridge acknowledged, while the rest of the crew continued their duties at their stations. A few minutes later, an announcement came that the rescue boat was in the water, headed toward the last known position of the crewman. The *Arisha*, now only visible by a few glimmering lights, faded into the darkness.

48

Hours had passed with no word from Angelina, Leonid, or anyone. The ship rumbled and rolled as it headed toward Russia. Left to the will of Vladislav, Ray faced the likely endpoint of his life and body. Convinced Angelina was probably dead, he felt he had one thing left to do.

He adjusted the power output and direction orientation of his GG device that had previously turned the ship and pressed it into the sea. His plan was to clamp it in the vise as before. Orienting it toward the ship's keel would do the necessary damage needed. Surely the *Arisha* would either sink by a breach or be dragged under by force. He preferred to die at sea instead of at the hands of Vladislav or his father.

He placed the shiny metal donut-shaped device into a small backpack he found under his bed. Since he didn't have a switch, he added what batteries he had and planned to hold the wires together or twist them quickly to activate the device when ready.

He sat up on his bed, stared at the door, and visualized the route back to the shop. It would be a difficult crawl, since he had no crutches. Angelina apparently wasn't able to find any on-board, and Vladislav had found it unimportant to bring them from his home. He needed to walk somehow. Could he make a splint for his foot in the cast? He gazed at the two wooden chairs with about two-inch diameter legs. He grabbed the closest chair, raised it over his head and smashed it against the steel floor. It bounced hard. The impact against the floor vibrated through the chair into his hand, causing pain like an electrical shock.

He changed the angle of his approach, lifting the chair again, this time letting go just before the chair struck the floor. The chair bounced, then rested. Picking it up and examining it, he noticed a hairline crack. Lifting it again, he threw it down. A leg flew off, breaking at the chair's base. He threw the chair again, and another leg broke free.

He gathered the two chair legs and placed them against his left ankle, one on each side. He scanned the quarters for something to fasten them to his leg. Then he noticed a familiar round gray object. A nearly full roll of duct tape lay on the floor. After tearing off long strips, he wrapped the chair legs around his loose pants. After several wraps of the tape, he placed weight on the leg. His pants shifted up, pain raced through his ankle, and he fell to the floor. *How stupid.*

After the pain subsided, he tore his pant leg fabric and taped the wood splints now to his bare skin. It didn't look well engineered, but the cast couldn't support his weight, so this was the best he could do. This contraption would not need to come off when he was dead, so it didn't matter. Standing again, placing weight on the makeshift brace, it held without the aggravating pain of his broken ankle. Quickly, he put on the backpack, stepped out the door, and trudged down the passageway.

At each doorway and corner, he checked for crew and saw none. When he reached the freight elevator, he pressed the button and waited. The door opened; an empty pallet sat on the floor. Stepping over the pallet, he rested his splinted foot on it, and pressed "1" for the floor he recalled from the earlier test. The door opened, the noise louder than the lone engine still pushing the *Arisha* along through the sea. He stepped out, walked past three passageways, and opened the familiar door into the shop. He shut and secured it, twisting the lock, not even sure it was a working lock.

Limping to the metal table next to the vise he'd used before, he removed the backpack, huffing. Carefully spilling the components onto the steel table, he quickly set the GG device into the vise, tightening it until it was secure, like before. He glanced at it, confirming the orientation of the device, paused, and thought. This should sink the ship or blow a hole in the bottom. He set the batteries on the table and connected the first of the two wires, twisting them securely. Then he recognized a problem.

When Tessa's kidnapper, Viktor Mishkin, launched his stolen GG device, the battery had separated. With all power to the stones removed, it fell into the San Francisco Bay. He needed to secure the power to the device if it were to move. He scanned the room full of large and small power tools, fixed wrenches, and hammers. Then he noticed a box of C-clamps. He carefully hobbled over, took two of the clamps, and returned to the vise. He placed the battery assembly against the side of the shiny donut shape, tightening each clamp one at a time, and switched back and forth, testing it to be sure it was firmly in place.

He stared at the GG device – two wires hanging, one twisted in place connected to the battery assembly, the others dangling free. Gazing at his black, oily hands, he wiped them on his dirty pants, and leaned against the table. With one last thought about his life as he knew it, he said, "This is for you, Tessa." He paused, then added, "For you too, Angelina."

He placed the wires one in each hand. Holding them close, he paused again. After taking a long breath, he closed his eyes, pressed the two copper connections together, gave them a quick twist, and let go.

49

Coast Guard Commander Steven Chapman sat at his desk on the second floor of the District Command Center in Honolulu, the recently setting sun a vivid orange memory. He pored over reports from one of his cutters, the *Rush*, sent to intercept a Russian merchant vessel recently disabled and reports of a high-speed boat and man overboard. He picked up his phone and called his sector command center. A voice answered, "Sector command, watch stander Miles."

"This is Commander Chapman. How soon can we have another cutter assist *Rush*?"

"Sir, *Sherman* is available. Could be at sea in about twenty minutes."

"Have the commanding officer call me as soon as he's available."

"Yes sir."

Chapman hung up. A knock came at his door. "Yes."

The door opened and a man in beige pants, white shirt and thin black tie announced, "FBI Agent Augustine and a Tessa Holland to see you."

"Show them in." He stood behind his large oak desk. His petty officer stepped aside and gestured, showing Agent Augustine and Tessa in. He closed the door. Augustine held out his credentials.

"That won't be necessary, Agent. I know you were checked when you came on-site. Have a seat." He pointed at the two cushioned wooden chairs in front of his desk.

They all sat.

Chapman fanned out the reports on his desk like he was dealing cards. "Quite a mess we have going on here, wouldn't you say?"

"I'm sorry, Commander, but I'm not sure what you're referring to," Augustine replied.

Tessa rested both her hands in her lap, her lips pressed thin.

"The *Rush* has intercepted the *Arisha*, but while making maneuvers to intercept a high-speed inbound target, one of her crew fell overboard. Nighttime is the worst for an MOB, so I've called up another cutter, *Sherman*, to assist. I think they said one person was on board the inbound target."

"Sir," Agent Augustine interrupted.

"Yes."

"I think we know who the inbound target is."

Commander Chapman sat back in his high back leather chair. "Please, enlighten me."

"It's our Agent Hamilton. He purchased a boat from a charter company here, and we believe now he's trying to rescue Ray Holland."

"By himself? That's a death wish at night."

"We tried hailing him. He's not answering."

Chapman lifted one of the pages, slammed it down on his desk. "My report says he's not answering to anyone."

"Sir, has the *Sherman* left the dock yet?"

"Probably twenty minutes from now."

"Any chance we could be on-board?"

Chapman coughed softly then glanced back and forth at them. "I'll allow it, but *Sherman*'s commanding officer has the final say. You would only be observers. You follow orders and stay out of the way."

"Thank you, commander." Augustine stood.

"I'll have my petty officer drive you to the dock. The crew will situate you with all the necessary gear."

The commander's phone rang. Asking them to help themselves to the door, he picked up the phone. It was the commanding officer of the *Sherman*, Robert Willis. Chapman filled him in on the situation with *Rush* and the *Arisha*, the high-speed boat with an agent at the helm, and now the two observers. Willis - not pleased to have two observers on board, but respecting Chapman's request - approved.

50

Ray opened his eyes and swore, knowing something went wrong. He wasn't in heaven, that was for sure. After closely scanning the familiar setup, following each wired connection, each circuit component, he noticed movement. A capacitor that shouldn't be moving. Looking closer, he saw the broken solder joint between the capacitor and the board. It was one he had clipped off the other larger GG power control board. The pin hadn't passed completely through the electronic breadboard.

He needed to go get the soldering iron, bring it back to the shop to repair it, then try again. He untwisted one pair of wires from the D pack of batteries, letting them dangle loosely. Then he stood, placing some weight on his foot with the chair legs still taped in place. Like a pirate with a wooden leg, he carefully hobbled to the door of the shop and down the passageway to the freight elevator. Pressing the button, he waited. The elevator ground and churned as it approached his floor. The doors opened empty again, and he breathed a sigh of relief. Stepping inside, he pressed the button for his floor, the door shut, and the churning started up again.

When the elevator stopped, the door opened to two men facing him. It was Vladislav and someone he didn't recognize. Vladislav gazed at Ray, his greasy dirty clothes, the makeshift crutch on his leg. He grabbed him by the collar and threw him into the passageway where he crumpled to the floor.

"Mr. Holland, why are you not in your quarters?"

"What have you done with Angelina?" Ray growled.

"You, Mr. Holland, should not be concerned with my Angelina. You should be concerned about your life and that of your wife. I ask again, why are you not in your quarters?"

Ray looked up from the floor, searching for an answer that wouldn't get him kicked while completely vulnerable. "I was looking for parts for the stone device."

Vlad turned to the other man next to him, said something in Russian, then the man walked down the passageway out of sight.

Vladislav scowled. "Leonid was to help you with anything you needed."

"I don't understand Russian, and Leonid doesn't understand English."

"I don't believe you. This is not why you move about my ship. There is no escape, you know."

"I'm not trying to escape. I need parts."

"I still don't believe you." He drew his foot up to stomp on his groin.

Ray turned, raised his leg, blocking the blow, and groaned as the Russian's boot pounded against his thigh. Vladislav lifted his foot again and kicked him in the butt. "Get up. We're going back to your quarters."

Ray rolled into a crawl, used his now-sore good leg to lift himself to a stand, and hobbled down the passageway. The other Russian crewman appeared carrying a brass padlock, latch, cordless drill, and bolts. Ray made his way to his quarters and opened the door. As he stepped inside, Vladislav shoved him. He fell to the floor. The door slammed closed, the latch clanged, then he heard the whine of a drill, metal against metal. More pounding and grinding of metal continued for several minutes, then silence.

After about twenty minutes, Ray stood, made his way to the door, and lifted the latch to open it. It would unlatch, but something outside was keeping it from opening. Probably a padlock, he suspected. *Now what?* He was stuck. *Maybe no more food until they dock in Russia.* He wobbled unsteadily to his bed, lay down, and buried his face in his pillow, contemplating how his death would come. He soon fell asleep.

51

Clang, clang, clang echoed in the quarters. Ray opened his eyes and rolled onto his side, facing the door. He twisted to sit up. He grimaced as his thigh and butt reminded him of Vladislav's boot. Another clang, metal against metal. *What's going on?* Were they barricading him in further? When it came time to remove him, what would they do – use a cutting torch to get to him? Another bang, this time followed by a clatter. He heard a voice outside, then silence, just the rumble of the constant diesel engine pushing the *Arisha* along.

Ray waited, then crawled to the door and checked the latch. It released, and this time the door opened. On the floor was a broken padlock and a drop of what looked like blood next to a shiny steel tray. In the tray were D batteries, spools of copper wire, wire cutters, solder, flux, and a soldering iron. It also held a hard bread roll, two bottles of water, a can of soup, and a piece of clothing with writing on it. He slid the tray in and shut the door, latching it. He took a bite of the roll, then swigged down half a bottle of water.

He froze and whiffed the air. Something familiar again. He lifted the cloth to his nose. It was Tessa's scent, but it couldn't be. Spreading the dirty cotton cloth on the floor, he studied the large writing. Dark drawn images, lettering on both sides of the irregularly shaped cloth. Someone had torn it from something. He flipped it back and forth, trying to make sense of what he was seeing. Lines, crossing lines, squares, and circles. Then just three words, "Come to me." Could this be from Angelina hiding somewhere on the ship? The lines had to be a map. Impossible. There was no way he could do this without being seen.

It could only be Angelina who broke his lock and brought the things he needed to complete the other GG device capable of getting them off the ship. Although...off a ship in the middle of the ocean. He still had a serious problem, and time was against him. He had the components to complete and test the other remaining GG unit. Vlad would be back again. Now, seeing the lock broken, the Russian would just re-lock the door once he verified he was there.

After taking a couple ibuprofen to soften his sore calf, he went to work. He placed all the components on the table, quickly mixing the orientation of the stones in the first half of the donut-shaped shell. Since the stones had previously been marked, the orientation completed quickly. He moved onto the second half, then assembled the two halves. Checking his math calculations to confirm what he estimated would be the lift variable he needed, he adjusted the two potentiometers and two variable capacitors.

Checking and double checking each solder joint with his tester, within two hours, he was ready to try it. Confident nothing bad would happen, he duct-taped the shell to the underside of the remaining unbroken chair, then sat on it. He soldered the first set of wires, wrapping them in tape. Without hesitation, he briefly tapped the remaining two wires together, completing the power circuit. The chair suddenly jumped but remained relatively stationary. This confirmed that he had removed the polarity component by balancing the orientation of the stones. He held the wires together longer, trying to compensate for the rolling of the ship, nearly falling off the chair twice.

Since he confirmed it would lift his weight and hold it, he wondered about adding Angelina's weight. It would need to carry both of them to safety. How long would the series of eight D cell batteries last and stay dry at sea? Duct tape was all he had. The eight D batteries would have to be enough. It was time to find Angelina. Packing the GG device, battery assembly, and duct tape into the backpack, he was ready to go. Only really knowing the way to the shop and storeroom, he studied the cloth drawing while finishing the roll, cold canned soup and drinking the remaining water.

He opened the door, standing with his broken chair legs still taped on, looked at the map, then turned right. Clumsily, he moved down the passageway, and soon he stood at a stairwell. It began to make sense, relating to the squares drawn on the map. Three squares. Either three steps or three floors up. It had to be three floors, as each floor had six stairs. He pulled on the handrail with each step of his right leg, pivoting for his left. He made slow progress.

On the third landing, he entered another passageway, long and brightly lit. He stared at the drawn circle on the cloth then noticed a welded circular cover on the floor. Feeling this was correct, he moved on, wobbling as quietly as he could. Following the line a few steps, he stopped again. *Now what?* He flipped the cloth over, trying to reorient the layout, when he caught a glimpse of something on the floor. Placing his shoulder against the wall for stability, he squatted, grimacing at the pain. It was a black line with an arrow pointing ahead. He reoriented the map to match the line.

Maybe this was a point where Angelina was sure he would get lost. She was right. He rose clumsily and followed the direction of the arrowed line. He arrived at a two-step stairwell, which brought him to a long, dark, rusty passageway, apparently not maintained well or traveled much. The musty smell of rotting iron and salt air resonated in this pathway. Careful to keep his braced leg quiet, he moved slowly down the long passage. It dead-ended at a sealed door with a circular crank-type handle, resembling those he'd seen on wartime movies on ships. He turned it until the door flexed and pulled it open.

The space inside was dark, but the air felt dryer against his face. It smelled more of fresh paint than that of rusting iron.

Glancing at his make-shift map, the last of the drawn lines ended. He could see by the contour of the wall he was near the outside hull of the ship. He continued down the service-like path, which had a handrail that allowed him to ease the weight on his left leg. After ten minutes on this single pathway, he arrived at another door with a circular crank handle. He rotated it, but it only turned a quarter and stopped hard. *Now what?* Where was Angelina? Using his knuckle, he knocked, and whispered, "Angelina."

He heard a screech of metal; the handle began to turn on its own. He froze, unsure who was coming. Looking back, the way he came to escape if needed, but against anyone with two working legs, he was no match. The door opened into darkness, an arm reached out and pulled him into the blackness.

52

Stumbling, he fell to the cold steel floor. The door shut with a clunk. He heard the sound of the handle spinning, followed by the grind of metal against metal, then another clunk. Suddenly, the room lit up, and he raised his hand to cover his eyes. A face streaked with dirty smudges, the ear still wrapped in a dried blood gauze, Angelina smiled. Pulling him to a stand, she threw her arms around his neck and grasped him tight, then kissed his neck over and over. After a long moment, she slowly released her grip. They faced each other.

"I thought you were dead," he said.

She immediately pulled him close again, kissed him passionately on the lips, and held it until he returned the kiss with the same enthusiasm. His heart pounded hard, glad to have found her alive. Someone on this ship who cared about him. He glanced down at his chest, wondering if she could feel the strong beats of his heart. Then he noticed red blood amongst the dirt and grime of her sleeve. Grabbing her forearms, he held them out, twisting them back and forth, searching for the source. He slid his hands out to hers, felt her left hand. Her hand was swollen, sticky, encrusted in dried blood.

He gently felt three fingers inside the loose cloth wrapping. She flinched.

"Oh my God, what happened?" he gasped.

"Vlad," she whimpered.

He growled. "How could he? This goes beyond being a monster. He is truly vicious."

"This is nothing. He will kill me if he finds me. This is why I'm here."

He glanced around the room. "I'm lost. Where is here?"

"I don't know its name, but no one comes here. I have food and water, even a bed." She pointed into a V-shaped corner where a couple of small, thin mattresses lay folded like a hammock.

Angelina lifted Ray's backpack off and led him onto the bed. Then she noticed his chair-pegged-leg. She smiled. Does that hurt?"

"Nothing compared to Vlad's boot into my thigh."

"At least he didn't cut you."

Ray grimaced when he sat in the V-shaped concoction of mattresses, so Angelina laid him gently back, then snuggled up next to him.

"Can I look at your hand?" He turned his face, taking in the greased features of her cheek and chin. With his thumb, he wiped a grease streak on her cheek, only spreading its smear.

She held her hand out; he slowly removed the wrapped cloth. His body shivered as he caught sight of the mostly missing middle finger at the second digit. A clean cut at the joint, white bone exposed, the skin and muscles tattered. Holding his breath a moment, he concentrated on Angelina's face to settle his queasiness. She held up a roll of gauze from a first aid kit and handed it to him. He gently re-wrapped her hand and stubbed finger.

"You're going to need a hand surgeon."

She grasped his arm with her right hand, squeezed and asked, "We go to America; you can help me?"

"Getting to America? I wish it was that easy."

Angelina rolled on top of him. He sank further into the folded bedding.

"We can get to America. You are smart. Your device can carry us away."

"Angelina. I'm not sure it will work." Ray paused. "I need to tell you something, something important. I thought you were dead. I gave up hope and went to the shop like we did before. I set my device to sink the ship, but it didn't work. In my rush to reconfigure it, I made mistakes. Then Vlad found me. That's when he kicked me. At that moment I so wished the ship was sinking."

He pointed to the backpack. "Now this device... I quickly tested it, but it may not carry us far. We don't know which way to go. When the batteries die, I can't swim. We both will probably drown. We're in the middle of the Pacific Ocean, headed to Russia. A madman on board wants to kill us both. America seems so far away right now."

She unbuttoned his shirt with her right hand and stroked his temple with her loosely bandaged left hand. After lifting off her grimy shirt to nothing underneath, she unlatched Ray's belt.

"What are you doing?"

"*Motivatsiya.*" She smiled.

"This doesn't change our situation."

"No, but I will not die without hope, nor will I die a coward." Without climbing off the bed, Angelina removed her thin pants, slipped off her underwear, then drew Ray's pants down to his taped, pegged leg. She gently pulled them free, leaving the taped wood in place.

"Maybe we should —"

"Shhh," Angelina interrupted, pressing her naked body on top of him and kissing him passionately on the lips. He placed both hands on her warm back, carefully drew her tight, and grimaced.

Angelina pushed her weight off his chest, feeling him tensing. "Am I hurting you?"

"No, no, it's just my hip where Vlad..."

"Ah, I will fix." She rolled off his naked body. She placed one leg above Ray's left hip, then set the other, carefully pushing down on his groin. Ray moaned.

"That better?"

"Yes, but..."

"Shhh." She lay forward on his chest, finding his lips again.

53

The *Arisha*'s dark stern loomed above a churning sea, casting a shimmering reflection of starlight on the moonless night.

Wiping the cold, salty spray from his face, Hamilton pulled back the throttle, flipping two switches and darkening all the lighting on the rigid inflatable. This was his opportunity to approach the *Arisha*, so far unnoticed. He held binoculars with night vision to his face with one hand and scanned the *Arisha*'s stern for a crewman on watch. He smiled, seeing none. Grasping a gaff hook with a line attached, he hoped his boat's insignificant blip on the radar screen had gone unnoticed.

Everything was working to his plan, and he was particularly encouraged after having earlier seen a US Coast Guard vessel nearby. That made his success more likely. He would soon be a courageous hero to Tessa when he rescued Ray, her husband –if he was alive. He was confident things could all work out. Tessa had provided signals of attraction to him, and alienated feelings for Ray. This rescue would seal the deal. *I'm the genuine man she needs in her life.*

He glanced behind the rigid inflatable and scanned the horizon, looking for the Coast Guard cutter. Spotting it well to the south behind him, brightly lit against the dark starry sky, he couldn't make out if they were approaching or not. Not being familiar with night navigation, the colored lights and arrangements on ships and boats meant nothing to him other than their presence nearby. He noticed another ship farther to the southwest. Its narrow shape revealed it was headed either toward him, or away. Again, it really didn't matter, it was time. He gently sped up until he bumped up onto the port side of the ship's stern.

Flipping a small lever on the console, he locked the steering to hold the boat against the *Arisha's* hull. Its inflated rubber side bounced, splashing seawater onto his face. The saltwater burned his eyes, so he paused, waiting to clear his vision. Then he whirled the gaff hook like a rodeo cowboy. Several times he let it circle so he could gauge its weight and the timing of its release. Confident in the direction and distance, he released it upward toward the obscure railing of the ship. It clanged, bounced cleanly off, and fell into the sea behind him. He pulled it back, his hands quickly saturated through his fingerless gloves.

As the hook drew close, the inflatable boat bounced hard against the *Arisha*, and he stumbled. A metal against metal clang sounded. The radar frame had struck the *Arisha's* hull as they rolled in a wave. He righted himself and finished retrieving the line and hook. Readying again, he took aim and gave another throw. Again, a miss. He cursed. *If pirates can do this, I can*, he assured himself. On his third throw, the line went over the rail and caught.

He grinned at his success. He pulled to set the hook and tied the line to the starboard forward cleat. He would need the boat for his escape if unsuccessful at taking control of the ship. He wasn't sure how many crew members would be armed on a merchant vessel, but he was FBI, trained in using the two Glock 23s he was carrying.

He shut off the engines with a turn of the key, the inflatable now towed by the *Arisha*. Suddenly, a horn sounded, then a voice boomed over a ship's paging system – Russian words he didn't understand. The *Arisha* lit up, her aft deck lights bright on the stern. He heard shouts. His luck was over. They'd discovered him. Racing forward to grab the line to start his climb of twenty feet of free-board, he looked up to see a shadow.

A shout, a flash, the crack of a gun fired in his direction. Diving in close to the ship, out of the line of fire, his weight tipped the rigid inflatable toward the hull of the *Arisha*. The hardened aluminum frame scraped hard against the massive ship. It wasn't giving back with each bounce of a wave against the ship's side. He had to move. Another shot rang out, striking metal. He needed to balance the boat, or it would roll. Each dip tipped the inflatable toward the hull of the *Arisha*. The radar frame crashed against the massive ship, and the module shattered and fell into the sea.

He heard more shots over the crashing of aluminum against steel, but he was being thrown back and forth as the boat bounced. He reached for his Glock, hoping he could get a shot off to show whoever was shooting he was armed as well, maybe subdue the fire so he could work at getting the rigid inflatable stable again. Soon the physics of water and weight were too much, the skiff rolled completely over, throwing him against the hard steel hull and into the dark, churning sea.

54

The bridge of the US Coast Guard cutter *Sherman* was dark, only illuminated by a dull, red glow. Square screens displayed her position relative to multiple blips on the screen, some with an identification name or number. Two rows of crew stations filled the crowded bridge. Men and women monitored navigation information, depth soundings, ship's speed, wind speed and direction, and weather information.

Tessa and Agent Augustine observed from the side of the bridge, instructed to stay out of the way. Commanding Officer Robert Willis and Officer of the Deck Findley stood side by side in the middle of the bridge scanning the dark sea with binoculars. A Coast Guardsman stepped forward, dressed in his blue uniform, and announced, "*Rush* recovered the MOB and is headed to *Arisha*."

Tessa overheard the information and whispered to Agent Augustine, "Does this mean we turn around?"

"Hard to say. With Agent Hamilton out here, both ships may stay, particularly now that it's dark."

Findley stepped back, walking back out of sight to the second row of stations. She came back a moment later.

"Twenty minutes to *Arisha*. No sight of the RIB on the radar. Tracking indicated an intercept of *Arisha*."

Willis rubbed the back of his neck with his hand. "How long ago did the intercept occur?"

Findley stepped away for a moment, returning a moment later, and answered, "one hour."

Willis turned and glanced briefly at Tessa and Augustine. "Maybe he was able to reach the *Arisha* and is on board."

Findley stood rigid. "He may have been discovered and was disabled or sunk."

An announcement came over the radio, "Bridge, radar contact zero-nine-zero, range two miles, stationary, possible small boat."

Willis turned to face Findley, rubbed his chin. "That may be the missing RIB. Turn to heading zero-nine-zero, slow ahead,"

Findley verified the course change with the helmsman.

Another announcement came, "Bridge, radio contact PLB, one-three-one, range four miles."

"Helm, turn to heading one-three-one, standard ahead," Willis ordered.

Again, Findley verified the course change with the helmsman. Willis turned toward Tessa and Agent Augustine. "PLB would be a personal locater beacon. Looks like we may have found your agent."

Tessa tried to smile, but recognized this could be a body recovery. Augustine reached around Tessa's shoulder and gently pulled her to him in a reassurance hug. She looked at him, her lips pressed thin.

"Trust me. I hope he's alive so I can pound some sense back into him," Augustine said.

A shout came from the port side of the bridge from the junior OOD, "Beacon, ten degrees to port, one-thousand yards."

Commander Willis responded, "Helm, turn to heading one-two-seven, slow ahead. Officer of the Deck, launch a rescue boat."

Findley coordinated the launch from the second row of the bridge. The rescue boat with three on board was successfully enroute in less than five minutes.

An announcement came to the bridge of the *Sherman*. "Bridge, radio, one person recovered from the water, unconscious male, CPR in progress."

Tessa heard the announcement and gasped. She covered her mouth and pressed her face into Agent Augustine's shoulder. He held her tight.

"How soon to recover the rescue boat?" Willis asked Findley.

"Five minutes."

"Once the person is on board, send the rescue boat to check the RIB for anyone else in the water or on board, just in case."

Findley verified the order, stepped back to the second row of stations to pass the orders to her crew.

For twenty tense minutes, Tessa and Agent Augustine stood by, waiting for information on the man found in the water, presumably Agent Hamilton. Commanding Officer Willis approached and pointed to the door off the bridge. "Your agent is alive and in the medical ward. He swallowed a bunch of sea water. Looks like death warmed over, but I suspect he'll recover."

Tessa's legs gave out and she fell into Augustine's arms as he exhaled deeply.

Willis led them down a passage, then down two flights of stairs. They could hear coughing and swearing as they approached an open door. On a raised medical bed was Agent Hamilton, white blankets covering him. His eyes were swollen almost closed, his face pale, and he coughed and spit into a light blue medical basin. Hamilton made eye contact, first with Tessa, then with Agent Augustine. He frowned.

Willis excused himself and headed back to the bridge. The attending medical technician followed.

"What were you thinking?" Augustine asked. "Looks to me like piss poor planning."

Tessa stood rigid, silent, with one hand holding onto Augustine's red Coast Guard-provided jacket.

Struggling to get the words out without coughing, Hamilton rasped, "I was there. Hooked the ship. Only steps away from being on board."

"What happened?" Augustine asked.

"Someone saw me. Opened fire... I took cover... boat rolled hard into... ship. Launched me in prop wash." He stopped to cough again. "Remember coming up, lungs burning... under again, then nothing. Till I heard a voice, pressure on my chest, a woman's face."

Augustine pulled his arm away from Tessa's grip. "Stay right here for me. I need a word with Hamilton."

Tessa gazed at the agent, ran both hands through her hair, and glared, but remained frozen in place.

Augustine walked to the bed and leaned in close to Hamilton's face. "What you did to Tessa was out of line, unprofessional, and shameful. This will probably end your career in the Bureau, and your life might be over when your sister gets hold of you."

"You don't understand. She consented," Hamilton said in a low voice.

"If she consented, you're obscene and cruel. I spoke with her ER doctor at the hospital. This doesn't look consensual, plus she's a married woman. Where's your moral value, code of ethics? Everything about this looks bad, and you won't hang one bit of it on me. If she presses charges, I won't defend you."

Hamilton's eyes glossed over; a small tear appeared. He spoke loud enough for Tessa to hear. "I'm in love with Tessa. I needed to know if Ray was dead or alive. I was willing to risk my life to know."

"And if Ray is alive, then what?" Augustine growled loud enough for Tessa to hear. "How would you explain to him what you did to Tessa?"

Tessa burst from her stance and pushed by Agent Augustine. She pounded on Hamilton's chest with both fists, screaming, "Why, why, why would you do this to me?" She collapsed onto his chest.

He coughed, then gently reached his arms around her as she wept.

55

The sky wore a wash of orange popcorn clouds as the sun peeked above the east horizon. On the *Arisha*'s bridge, Captain Semenov observed the two American Coast Guard ships drawing close in the settling seas. Vladislav stepped onto the bridge. Semenov and his junior officer, Elin, at the helm, made eye contact, then resumed their duties.

"What of this attack on my ship?" Semenov scowled at Vladislav.

"One man in a small boat not much of an attack, only a fool. The American Coast Guard would not be so foolish. He's gone now, so we keep our heading."

Semenov pointed and swept his hand toward the horizon. "The American ships, two of them now, continue to hail us, wanting us to stop and be boarded."

"Until they get word from their State Department, they will keep their distance."

"What then?"

Vladislav gave an evil smile. "Then my American guest will be food for creatures of the sea, I'm afraid."

"What of your father if you kill this American?"

"He will understand. The loss of this man compared to the loss of this ship and me to the hands of Americans. He will forgive me."

The VHF Radio on the bridge crackled, then a call sounded. "*Arisha, Arisha, Arisha*, this is Coast Guard Vessel *Sherman*. Halt and prepare to be boarded." The message repeated.

Semenov glared at Vladislav. "It looks like your time is up."

"Not possible." Vladislav picked up the radio. "*Sherman*, this is *Arisha*. You have no authority to board this ship in international waters. Leave us."

The radio crackled again. "*Arisha*, we understand you have an American prisoner on board; therefore, halt and prepare to be boarded."

Captain Semenov watched the *Sherman* through his binoculars, as it moved closer on the starboard side of the ship, matching the *Arisha*'s speed. Then the large auto cannon on the bow of the ship turned, pointing toward the *Arisha*.

"They are ready to fire upon us," he yelled to Vladislav.

Junior Officer Elin's eyes opened wide, waiting at his helm position for orders to come. Then he shouted to Semenov in Russian that the other American ship was now following within five-thousand yards.

Semenov went outside the bridge on the starboard side, and fixed his binoculars on a narrow shape coming toward them. Another announcement came over the VHF radio. This time, it included the words "be fired upon." Semenov directed his attention back to the *Sherman* just as smoke blew from the 76mm cannon on the bow. The boom followed immediately. A splash and explosion of water shot out of the sea fifty yards off their bow.

"I'm afraid your time is up," Semenov shouted to Vladislav.

"Hold them off!" Vladislav ran out the bridge door toward the steel stairwell.

Semenov gave the command in Russian to Elin to slow the ship.

56

As Vladislav rounded the corner of the bright passageway, a boom rocked the ship, and he stumbled. The rumbling of the one working diesel engine slowed. He was out of time. When he reached Ray's quarters, he saw the brass lock on the floor of the passageway. Broken pieces littered the area around the door, and the door hung open. Glaring inside, he hoped Ray was still there, but the quarters were empty. A stainless-steel tray sat on a table, a broken chair was splayed on the floor. Then he noticed the empty soup can, crumbs, empty water bottle, solder, wire, and iron.

"Impossible," he whispered as he scanned the room. "Angelina." He cursed. He hadn't seen her since a chance encounter in the passageway near Holland's quarters, a tray of food in her hands. She had used the tray of food to shield herself from his knife, managing to dodge his attack, but not without harm. She then made a run for it, leaving him slipping and falling on the mess of food on the deck.

Holland…he couldn't do anything for her… or could he? This far out to sea, not a chance. He ran down the passageway until he found a crewman in the mess hall eating. Yelling at him to follow him, he led him to Ray's former cabin and instructed him to clean up the mess immediately. Making his way down to the engine room, now idle, he ordered the crew to assist in the search for Ray and Angelina. He told them to spread the word that if the American officers boarded *Arisha*, there was to be no mention of Ray ever being on board.

Vladislav tripped as he entered the bridge. Gripping his knee, he grimaced, breathing hard from charging up the stairwell. Semenov's binoculars focused on the small inflatable approaching his ship, which now rocked gently in the rolling waves.

"The American is gone," Vladislav said, huffing.

"You fool, the Americans are approaching. They will see his body in the water."

"No, you fool. He is not in his quarters. He is somewhere on the ship. Likely with Angelina. No one is to speak of his being here."

Semenov growled, "I don't like lying for you. I only do it for the ship and crew."

"Good." Vladislav smiled, still breathing hard. "Did you radio Moscow of this action of the Americans?"

"In time, maybe you can. In only moments, we will deal with armed American officers. You should surrender your guns to them before they shoot you."

"I only need one to do away with the American and Angelina."

"You're an evil man, Vlad. I will be glad when you are off my ship. Your soul only breathes death and hardship."

Vladislav bared his teeth in a grin. "Maybe I will be rid of you when we reach port. I will be captain of *Arisha*."

"I will gladly part from this ship and its curse upon the sea," Semenov growled. "But I remain captain. You should obey my orders."

Shouts came from outside the bridge; clanging sounds from steel steps and chain handrails resonated. An officer in a bright orange vest, a blue cap, and holstered gun appeared.

"Who is Captain Semenov?" he demanded.

"I am Semenov." He turned toward and addressed him.

"You speak English."

"Yes, but not my crew."

"I am officer Matthews of the US Coast Guard." He handed Semenov a sheet of paper. Vladislav moved in closer to read it. It was in both English and Russian. A second officer dressed in the same bright vest and blue cap, stepped onto the bridge.

"This is an order allowing us to board your ship and perform a search and safety inspection." Matthews pointed to the other officer. "This is Yeoman Balan. She can translate for us."

Another armed officer wearing protective gear and carrying an assault rifle joined the scene on the bridge. He took a position near the rear of the bridge, an Ak47 held across his chest.

"I will need to see your ship's papers," Matthews ordered.

Vladislav stepped forward, waving the document the American officer had handed to his captain. "This is not valid at sea, only in American waters."

"Who are you?" Matthews asked.

"I am First Officer Vladislav."

"You speak English. Good. The enforcement document is valid and enforceable when we suspect a crime has been committed."

"What crime? We are a simple merchant vessel, conducting business in America."

Then Matthews' gaze fell on service weapon hanging in Vladislav's shoulder holster. "You will need to surrender your weapon while we are on board your ship."

Vladislav frowned, then slowly removed his Glock 19 from its holster, keeping it pointed to the deck, and handed it to Matthews, who passed it to his maritime enforcement specialist standing guard.

"Any other weapons on board or armed crew?" Matthews asked.

"Vlad is only crew who has gun," Semenov offered.

"Good," Matthews answered. "You will need to stay on the bridge while we conduct our search and safety inspection. Do you understand?"

Vladislav bristled. "I ask again. What crime have we committed?"

"We understand there may be an American prisoner on board. I hope for you, your ship, and your crew this isn't true." Matthews gave a hand gesture to his yeoman to follow him off the bridge.

57

Ray opened his eyes, and his body warmed as he gently passed his palm over Angelina's tangled blond hair and slick, bare skin.

Angelina stirred, opening her blue eyes to the brightness of their hidden space. An eerie silence loomed.

"I don't remember it being this quiet." Ray ran his finger across Angelina's forehead.

"The engine has stopped again."

He frowned. "What does this mean?"

"Shh... Listen." She tipped her head up. "That is crew yelling."

"What are they saying?"

"*Der'mo*," she whispered. "They are looking for us."

Pushing off Ray's chest with both hands, she winced, then stepped onto the steel floor, hurried to the door, and slapped the lights off with her right hand.

"Angelina," Ray whispered.

"Shhh."

In the dark they listened as the voices continued to yell. Doors slamming, metal clanging. The sounds grew louder, followed by silence. Then the door mechanism turned and stopped as the metal rod prevented it from freeing the door. It rocked back and forth, followed by pounding and shouting. They both held their breath. The sounds quickly faded. Angelina flipped the lights back on.

"They come back soon," she whispered. "We must prepare, hide."

Ray sat up. "Where?"

Angelina pointed to all the bottled water, cans of soup, and hard rolls.

"We must throw these all below." She pointed to a gap between the side of the ship's hull and steel floor. "Quickly."

Ray climbed out of the awkward bed, stepped onto the cool steel floor, shivered, and then crawled toward the food and water. He passed the provisions one at a time to Angelina while she dropped them through the opening. They heard a splash after dropping each bottle and can.

"Is that the bilge?" Ray asked.

"Yes."

"Do we have time to get our clothes on?" He crawled around and grabbed his pants and shirt.

"No. If discovered, we die. Everything must go into bilge."

"Wait. Clothes, and the backpack?" He held up his garments. "If they find us here naked, there won't be any doubt what's taken place."

She reached down and placed her hand on his chin. "Either way is death for us."

He grabbed her forearm, gently pulled her close and kissed her. "Angelina. We need the backpack, the GG device, to escape."

Smiling, she stood, and slapped him on the butt. "You must find a place. Quickly."

She picked up one mattress and placed it against the hull, standing it upright, and resting it against the ship's framing above the hole to the bilge.

"This is where we will hide." She pointed to the mattress. "You will stand, hold our clothes, but I will place the other mattress over us." She pointed to a dirty canvas sheet with metal eyelets down each side and corner. Weaving a corded rope through the top two corners, she quickly tied one end to a framing corner high in the room against the hull.

"This will cover the mattresses and us."

Ray furrowed his brow briefly as he interpreted Angelina's words. "If we're caught, this will be pretty embarrassing."

"It will be short only if Vlad kills us quickly. Finding me naked with you. His rage will end our lives."

"Can I use some of the rope to hang the backpack above the bilge?"

Angelina gazed at the rope and ran out a measurement, using her arm's length. She placed the twine in her mouth, ground her teeth, and handed four feet to Ray. Holding the twine, Ray gazed at her.

"How did you do that?"

"Something I learned as a little girl. If we live, I'll tell you story."

"Remind me to be more careful when we kiss."

Angelina smiled, then laughed. "That too."

Ray tied the twine to the backpack, pushing it carefully through the opening, then made two square knots, and slid it as much out of sight as he could. Angelina scanned the room for any evidence of their presence. Finding none, she told Ray to get up and lean against the mattress, resting his foot and chair-legged crutch on the rigid framing, as flat as he could. Once he was in place, standing naked, holding a handful of clothes in both hands over his waist, she lifted the other mattress, and placed it over him.

"Can you hold this and the clothes?" She handed him one end of twine.

"Yes," was his muffled answer.

\# \# \#

Angelina took the canvas mat, covered it over the mattresses, running the twine through more of the framing as close to the mattresses as possible. Securing half the bottom, she pulled the twine tight. Looking up at the light bulb, she reached up, trying to loosen it, and snapped it back right away waving her fingers to cool them. Switching to her bandaged hand, she loosened it enough to remove it, and tossed it toward the opening to the bilge. A pop sounded as it shattered. She made her way to the door, slid the bar to block it, carefully adjusting it to fall at the slightest movement. She felt her way and found the mattress, canvas, and twine, and scooted in next to Ray. She secured the bottom with the twine, covering the mattress and all evidence of their presence.

Soon came muffled voices, a clang, then a slight creaking as the door opened. Something said in Russian concerning the lights. Angelina saw flashlight beams strafing across the ship's framing above the mattress opening. With only room for a few crew members, she knew only one or two would enter the space. She recognized a voice. It was Leonid Kotov, the second officer, her only trusted crew mate on board. He argued with the other crew, then ordered them out of the space and to search elsewhere. The door shut and they heard the handle turning, sealing the space once again. Angelina blew out a relieved breath.

"Can we get dressed now?" Ray asked, his voice muffled.

Angelina giggled. "Don't you like my nakedness?"

"I do, and the sex. Wow." He reached down and touched her midriff. "Maybe I'm just not as confident about mine."

Angelina released the twine holding the bottom of the canvas, kicking out the mattress covering them. It flopped silently to the floor. In the darkness she reached back, feeling Ray's leg, hip, arm, then hand, guiding him off the ledge. He stumbled. The clothes fell to the floor.

"How are you at dressing in the dark?" she asked.

Ray laughed. "As long as you wear yours and I wear mine." Angelina felt around, finding, then slapping his butt.

Carefully, they felt each piece of clothing, identified it, and handed them back and forth. After finding there were only two socks, they crawled around in the darkness, but could not find more.

Angelina found both of Ray's shoes, waved them around until they made contact with his body. "I'm sorry, no socks for you."

"More important, I found the rope with the backpack."

She Slapped her hand on the mattress on the floor. "Set it here while we get dressed. I'm afraid we can't stay here now."

"Can we get to the deck of the ship?"

"Yes, but we must climb a ladder."

"I can't do that with one bad foot, even with this makeshift splint."

Angelina crawled to the door, opening it slightly, letting in some light. They looked at each other, the grimy clothes, messy hair. Angelina smiled. "I will carry you up ladder."

"Angelina, I weigh one-hundred eighty-five pounds."

"I can do." She pulled down the canvas and twine that still hung against the hull of the ship, and folded it neatly, winding the twine around it. Ray stood, placing his weight on his good foot. Angelina reached around him and guided him out the narrow doorway.

58

United States Coast Guard cutters *Sherman* and *Rush* each flanked the *Arisha* as she powered up her one working engine, kicking up a wash of bubbles. She slowly moved away, turning east toward Russia. Officer Matthews reported back to Commander Chapman on the bridge of the *Sherman* via radio, stating they did not find any Americans on board the *Arisha* and that all documents were in order. After issuing a command for Matthews and his team to return to the *Sherman*, Chapman stepped off the bridge and made his way to the medical ward to pass the update to Tessa and the two FBI agents.

Hamilton lay, eyes closed, covered in thick white sheets. Tessa sat on a hard wood chair, her face in her hands. She sat up at the sound of hard soles on the linoleum floor. Peering up at Chapman, she quickly wiped away tears, her eyes red, swollen.

"We completed a search of *Arisha*. I'm afraid there was no sign of your husband."

Tessa covered her mouth, and new tears retraced salty paths down her cheeks.

She whimpered. "He's dead then?"

"We don't know that. Only that they did not find him in the search."

"Wait. What about the man and woman who kidnapped him?"

"The search reported no women on board either."

Agent Hamilton's eyes opened as he stirred. He cleared his throat and coughed once. "There was never a good ending to come of these Russian mobsters."

Tessa stood, stared at him, and yelled, "Is that so, Agent Hamilton? Maybe you should have disclosed this to me early on, before taking advantage of my vulnerability. Why even try to board a ship, knowing my husband was dead?" She sat down hard on the chair, her face flushed.

After a moment of eerie silence, Tessa looked at Commander Chapman. "What now?"

"As far as your situation with your missing husband, you'll have to file a missing person's report with the local agencies. As far as my duties are concerned, we will return to Honolulu so you can go back home. If you'll excuse me." Chapman turned and stepped out of the ward.

"I love you, Tessa. Whatever you need, I will take care of you."

Tessa stared back and furrowed her brow. "If I'm pregnant, I'll milk you for every penny possible." She stood and marched toward the door.

"We'll get married. It'll all be fine."

"Oh, shut up," she growled as she exited the ward.

59

Ray stared up at the rusty ship ladder, barely large enough for one person to climb because of the round steel casing surrounding it.

"Stay here." Angelina stepped onto the first bar. Carefully she placed each hand and foot, making her way to the top, which wasn't visible in the darkness. Ray heard grunting, then a noticed a thin bead of light. The same twine used to hold the canvas against the mattresses dropped, landing at Ray's feet. Angelina then carefully stepped down each rung until both feet rested back on the landing. Reaching around Ray, she folded the canvas sheet they had used before, and ran the twine through the eyelets, passing it around Ray's waist to create a harness.

"This isn't going to work." Ray said. "If I get stuck, you won't be able to escape."

Angelina, using her good hand, grasped Ray's shirt and pulled him close. "This will work. I'm not leaving without you." She placed her lips on his, holding for a long kiss.

Ray smiled at her confidence.

"When you get to the top, push hatch open, pull yourself out. You must do. Stay low."

"I can barely stand," he complained.

Angelina grinned. "Let us hope that is our only problem."

Lining Ray up, she used the rungs of the ladder to loop the rope as a makeshift pulley system to help lift upward and prevent him from falling back.

"Use your hands. I will pull."

Ray put one hand over the other, to lift himself up each rung, as Angelina took up the slack, and pulled down on the rope. With each step, Ray groaned as he kept catching his chair-legged crutch in every other step, but progress was being made. He winced when he hit his head on a latch handle, swore, then pushed the hatch open. Bright light filled the ship ladder, shadowed only by his body. Resting against the hatch cover, he shifted his hip onto its edge, clearing a path for Angelina. Once he caught his breath, he lay on his side on the rusty brown, peeling deck and untied the makeshift harness. Angelina passed the backpack with the GG device out of the hatch, squinting at the brightness of the mid-day sun.

Ray zipped open the backpack, setting the GG device on the deck. He tore off several strips of duct tape, applying them to the battery assembly, and adhered it to the side of the donut-shaped shiny housing. Continuing to pull more tape off the roll, he applied it, intending to make his device as waterproof as possible. He wrapped additional duct tape around the eight D batteries to ensure good contacts and reduce the chance of a break in the connection. All that remained was binding the wires to complete the power circuit.

"Angelina, I don't know if this will work in this environment. Salt water and electronics don't do well together."

Angelina took her bandaged hand and ran her thumb and forefinger across his cheek. "You are smart, you went to university, this will work."

"Remember, I can't swim. If I fall into the ocean, don't risk your life to save me. Save yourself."

"Stop." She poked her finger into his chest and glared into his eyes. "You save me, I save you."

Ray placed her hands on top of the GG unit, one on the inside of the donut shape and one on the outside.

"We each will hold on to it like this. If one of us gets tired, we can wrap our legs around the other person to relieve the weight."

Angelina gazed at Ray. "I will tire first." She held up her bandaged hand.

"We will hover in or above the water." He paused and peered into her eyes. "I'm not sure. If the GG device goes underwater, it may not hover, and we're done."

Angelina placed both her hands onto the taped-up gray device and nodded. "I am ready."

She stood, lifting Ray with her good hand. They leaned against the hard steel side of the ship, looking over the edge and down upon the slowly moving water. Then they noticed the two Coast Guard ships, one on each side of the *Arisha*, falling back as she pushed through the calm sea. Wind whipped Angelina's tangled dirty hair into her face. She brushed it back.

"Grab hold," Ray said.

Angelina placed her bandaged hand on the inside of the device, her good hand grasping the outside.

He connected the wires, completing the circuit. Angelina screeched as the GG unit jumped, but she held tight. Ray wrapped tape around the connection, then grabbed on as well. They looked over the edge, then at each other.

Shouts sounded from the direction of the *Arisha*'s bridge. They turned to see the crewmen scrambling about, some running down the stairwell toward them. Then suddenly the crack of gunfire, and sparks flew up from the deck near them.

Ray said, "Time to go."

They leaned over the rail and went headfirst toward the sea.

# # #

From the *Sherman*'s bridge, Commander Chapman used binoculars to watch his boarding team approach the ship's stern. The OOD on watch shouted out, "Commander, activity on the bow of the *Arisha*, possible gunfire!"

Commander Chapman focused his binoculars on the Russian ship. "What the hell. Radio Matthews. Send the team back toward the *Arisha*. Hail her, and helm, bring us around heading one-seven-zero."

The OOD called out with eyes locked in his binoculars. "Sir, two just went overboard off the bow of the *Arisha*. They're shooting at them."

"What? Inform Matthews, man overboard, man overboard, two in the water. Let the *Rush* know," Chapman ordered.

A horn wailed as the order came across the ship's PA system.

The OOD called out again, "Sir. Do you see this?"

"See what?"

"Four degrees off the bow just this side of *Arisha*. The two overboard aren't in the water, they're..." He paused a long moment. "Sir, they're walking on the water."

Commander Chapman scanned across the bluish gray sea against the dark shadow of the *Arisha* moving to port, then he saw them. "What the hell?" His mouth gaped.

60

Tessa, surrounded by mostly empty benched tables in the *Sherman*'s mess hall, took a bite of her hamburger. Not able to curb her anger and frustration, she turned to the only thing she knew to do, eat.

Agent Augustine sat across from her, two-handing a cup of coffee, as if his hands were cold. "Do you always eat like this?"

Wiping a dribble of catsup from her lip, she replied, "No," then took another bite.

"I remember my sister eating like that when she was..."

She flashed her hand into his face, stopping his words. "Don't say it. Don't you say it and ruin this moment. This brief moment of pleasure."

"Sorry, I was just..." he paused, "going to change the subject."

Tessa smirked, took another bite, and washed it down with several gulps of her Coke.

A horn sounded, followed by "Man overboard, man overboard." A few crew members in the mess hall jumped out of their seats and ran toward the exits. The ship turned and listed to port.

At the doorway stood Agent Hamilton, dressed in blue cotton pants and matching button-up shirt, dodging the outgoing crew.

Augustine looked him up and down. "The medical staff release you?"

"Yes. I heard you were down here. What's all the commotion?"

"Man overboard, it sounds like," Augustine said.

Tessa continued to eat.

"A drill?"

"I doubt it under the circumstances. Let's go have a look."

Tessa glanced at what remained of her burger, fries, and Coke, took one last sip, and followed the two agents.

A small Coast Guard boat approached the *Arisha*, and what sounded like gunfire erupted shortly after.

"Are they crazy, firing on a Coast Guard ship?" Hamilton put his hands on his hips.

"It looks like they're seeing something in the water." Augustine pointed. "Two people. Long hair, I'd say one is a woman. They are on something, or... holding onto something. Their feet are in the water, and it looks like they're running."

"A woman?" Tessa asked. "Chapman said there were no women on board. Would it be the Russian and his girlfriend? Why would they shoot at them?"

Then Tessa recognized a leg less mobile than the other on the man as he tried to run. "That's Ray. Has to be. They're hanging onto one of his GG devices."

"His what device?" Augustine asked, as Agent Hamilton stared in the direction of the two in the water.

Suddenly, one of the women's arms appeared to release its grip and dangled. She lifted her legs out of the water and wrapped them around the man.

The Coast Guard high speed inflatable raced toward the *Arisha*, as Officer Matthews fired shots from an MK18 assault rifle toward the incoming fire. The two in the water disappeared from view behind the *Arisha* as she steered away from the Coast Guard inflatable. More shots rang out from the *Arisha*.

#

Ray's left hand released its grip. Angelina's only good hand slipped. He strained at the extra load, moments away from drowning.

"Angelina. I can't hold us both," he panted.

She reached up, grabbed his raised arm with her good hand, gripped and pulled, shimmying her legs higher on his body. Now able to slap her right hand on the side of the GG device, she tried once more as the sea splashed about at Ray's feet.

"I can't feel my hand," Ray shouted. Blood trailed from his wrist down his arm.

She gasped. "You've been shot."

"I'm sorry, Angelina." His grasp released. They gently fell, swallowed into the dark sea. The GG device floated about in the light wind.

#

From the lower deck railing of the *Sherman*, now slowed and only producing a small wake in the rolling sea, Tessa watched the events unfold. "Ray can't swim," she screamed. Quickly placing one foot on the lower rail, she stepped over, and faced the sea thirty feet below.

"Don't do it," Augustine yelled, reaching for her, only able to slap her foot as she dove.

A pop-pop came from the bridge railing above. Augustine turned to look to see Hamilton firing his Glock toward the man and woman who were now splashing about. He was clearly out of accurate pistol range, not firing toward the *Arisha*. Augustine yelled, "Stand down, Hamilton, stand down!"

Hamilton kept firing until he exhausted his first clip. As he pulled out a spare clip, a Coast Guardsman in blue pants and bright orange jacket tackled him from behind. Pushing him first against the metal rail, the Guardsman then threw him hard onto the deck. A second Coast Guardsman secured the weapon as he helped hold Hamilton to the deck with his knee.

Out of breath, Augustine stepped up onto the bridge platform. "What the hell are you doing, Agent Hamilton?" he yelled.

"Get off me," Hamilton snarled at the two Coast Guardsmen holding his arms behind his back. A third Coast Guardsman approached with silver cuffs and pressed them in place. They pulled him to a stand, so he faced Augustine.

"Are you out of your mind?"

Hamilton's eyes glassed over, staring at the sea, but he said nothing.

Augustine turned, seeing Tessa swimming strong, now seventy yards from the *Sherman*, toward the splashing couple, still hundreds of yards away.

61

Ray bounced about, splashing his arms into the water, coughing, spitting, breathing hard. Facing Ray, whipping her long hair from her face, Angelina dove underneath him, coming up to face the back of his head. She reached her arm around his neck, held his chin up, and shouted into his ear, "Stop... Relax... Lay back... I have you."

Ray quit floundering. His chest floated to the surface as she pulled back and kicked her feet, dragging him through the water. Angelina scanned the sea, seeing the bright white ship off in the distance. Only the stern of the *Arisha* was visible, muffled gunfire echoing off the sea. Horns sounded as the ship launched another bright orange boat from her stern. Kicking and paddling with her one good arm and hand, she kept looking toward the white ship, when she noticed something swimming toward them. The swimmer approached, long black hair flowed behind with each crawl stroke. A woman. Then she heard a muffled voice, "Ray, Ray."

Who was this person who knew Ray? She continued to swim with strong kicks toward the ship. Knowing Ray's vulnerability, she was not stopping for anyone. As the woman drew close, she tried to grab Ray's shoulder, but missed, slipping behind him. Angelina was now able to look into the eyes of the stranger.

"Ray," the woman shouted. "It is you."

Ray opened his eyes, red from the salt water. "Tessa?"

"Ray. It is you," she shouted again, spitting out salt water. "Stop, stop." She took a quick breath. "I will take it from here."

Angelina continued stroking and yelled, "I will save him."

"That's my husband." The woman took another strong breath. "I will take it from here, whoever you are."

A muffled engine sounded in the distance, disturbing the lapping of the splashing sea against each stroke Angelina took.

"I am Angelina, and he is not your husband." She continued to stroke and kick as Tessa treaded water, falling behind them. Swimming to them, she reached and grasped Ray's dangling leg, slowing their progress.

"Leave him," Angelina shouted.

"No, you leave him."

"I have him. I will save him."

Tessa swam up next to Angelina, took a swing at her face, but missed.

Angelina changed direction, keeping Ray between her and Tessa.

Tessa growled and swam ahead of Angelina to intercept her path, but Angelina only turned away again.

A bright orange boat approached, the motor suddenly slowed, the wake splashing the three of them. Bringing the boat up to Tessa, a man reached out to pull her aboard. She leaned back out of reach.

"Get in the boat, ma'am," the young Coast Guardsman shouted.

"Not until my husband's on board."

"Get out of the way," Angelina yelled toward Tessa as she drew Ray in close. A Coast Guardsman reached down, grabbed Ray first by the collar, then under the arms, and pulled him on board. Using her good hand, Angelina reached up and was soon aboard.

Tessa offered her hand after seeing Ray was safe. Quickly a Guardsman seated and wrapped them in silver blankets and asked each their names. Ray held up his bleeding hand, which one of the Coast Guardsman examined immediately and wrapped in gauze. Angelina sat next to Ray. Tessa sat directly across the boat as it sped back toward the *Sherman*, radioing ahead that all three were aboard.

Angelina grabbed Ray's free hand with her good one. "We made it, we made it," then kissed his cheek.

Tessa stood, only to be pulled back down by a Coast Guardsman seated next to her. She shouted, "Get your hands off my husband!"

Angelina just grinned and pressed her bandaged hand on top of her other one in Ray's lap.

"Ray, who is this woman?" Tessa shouted over the roar of the engines.

Ray slowly looked up and gazed into Tessa's eyes. "Tessa, meet Angelina, the woman who saved my life."

"Wait, what? Who saved who here?" She yelled as she rang salt water from her dangling hair. "Ray, did you see I swam out here to save you from drowning? I dove off a moving ship. I believe this counts for something."

Ray continued to stare at Tessa. "I remember your last words in the hospital. You told me to leave."

# # #

The *Arisha* slowly drifted after being ordered to stop and prepare to be boarded for a second time. The gunfire had ceased. ME Matthew's team scrambled up the ladder and took control of the bridge. On the bridge side extension, they found a man dead, multiple holes seeping blood from his chest. His gun lay next to him. The bridge windows were shattered, glass fragments strewn about. Captain Semenov, Leonid Kotov, and Denis Elin stood on the bridge with their hands up, following the orders of the American Coast Guardsmen.

"Why would you fire on us, Captain?" Matthews asked, standing on the bridge, facing the three Russians.

"It was not I, only Vladislav Mishkin."

Matthews pointed to the dead man outside on the platform. "Your first officer, I recall."

"Yes. He is only one on board with a gun."

"Captain, we recovered a man and woman from the water. Had they been on board your ship?"

"Yes. He was prisoner of Vladislav. The woman, Angelina was with Vlad. You must understand, he threatened us, and his father owns this ship. We had no choice but to follow his orders."

"I'm afraid you are the ship's captain; therefore, you are responsible for the actions of the ship and crew. We are taking control of this ship and are returning it to Pearl Harbor. There, we will conduct a thorough search of the ship, collect evidence, and interview your crew. Once we complete these actions, we'll decide the fate of this ship and its crew."

62

Upon boarding the *Sherman*, Ray and Angelina were taken to the medical ward to attend to Ray's wrist and cast foot, as well as Angelina's hand and ear. Tessa was taken to quarters to get cleaned up and dressed. Once dressed in Coast Guard-provided blue cotton pants and button-up shirt, she waited in the ship's mess. She placed her hand to her cheek. The muscles in her face her were tight, and her skin crawled being separated from Ray. She needed to talk to someone, but who would listen and assure her this could all be fixed. Back to the way it was. *I need to talk to Ray, but not with that woman at his side.*

Agent Augustine stepped in, saw Tessa sitting alone, and sat down across from her.

"Well, so much for filing a missing person's report," Tessa offered.

Augustine chuckled. "The question becomes, now what?"

"I wish I knew."

"Well, all I can say is Hamilton's job at the Bureau is over, I'm afraid. Commanding officer Willis has made a list of charges against him. The worst being the unauthorized discharge of a weapon on board his ship. Willis refuses to hear about the possible love triangle and shooting at unarmed civilians."

"Love triangle." She laughed. "I really don't want to see him ever again, you know. Except when I see that woman... what's her name... Angelina? Then I want Hamilton to take her away, make her disappear. Maybe you can do that for me."

"I'm afraid Hamilton is being put on the first plane to San Francisco. He has some serious questions to answer from his superiors there. I'm sure he'll be released from his duties in the Bureau. As far as Angelina, if she's a Russian citizen, she's probably going back to Russia once a determination has been made regarding *Arisha* and her crew."

She held her arms out like she was going to hug someone. "Good. She can go back to Russia. Leave Ray and I to pick up the pieces, get on with our lives."

"You know he's going to call you. What are you going to tell him?"

"About?"

Augustine scrunched his forehead. "You know what about."

"He doesn't need to know."

"A DNA test will prove otherwise."

Tessa bit her lip. "Oh that. I'll cross that bridge if it comes to that."

"Can I give you some friendly advice?"

"No."

He spread his hands, palms up. "You should be up front with him. Get it out in the open."

"It'll be over if I do. I can't even explain what happened, how it happened." Her shoulders dropped as she bore the weight of her thoughts. *Why can't this be easy? Why can't I just say how I feel, and have everything be the way it should be?*

He placed his hand on her forearm. "The medical report is relatively straight forward."

"What? Regarding rape? There I said it again. He raped me."

"That's a messy court case if it comes to that. Trust me, I'm not standing up for him just because he's my brother-in-law. It's just one of those things that nobody wants to go through in court."

"I'm not going there. I just want Ray back."

Then she heard voices, turned, and watched Ray and Angelina walk into the mess hall, clean and dressed in the same Coast Guard blue T-shirt and pants. Angelina had her arm laced through Ray's free arm. His other hand used a cane to walk. Fresh bandages covered her ear, and her opposite hand was wrapped, clearly displaying the loss of two-thirds of her middle finger. Ray's foot was wrapped in a clean dressing and plastic boot cover. Angelina drew Ray in close when she glanced toward the pair seated alone in the mess hall.

Tessa curled her lip in a snarl. Agent Augustine reached for her left arm on the table and held it there, keeping her from standing.

Commander Willis arrived, along with two other officers, catching up with Ray and Angelina. He pointed to a table, and they all sat down.

Tessa heard introductions of the two man as part of his investigative team. She tried to stand again, but Agent Augustine held her arm.

"You won't be allowed as any part of that conversation over there," he said. "It's important that Ray explains the events that took place without a distraction."

"Are you calling me a distraction?"

"Yes. Right now, you are."

Tessa lifted her cooled coffee to her lips and sputtered when she saw Angelina snuggle into Ray's shoulder. "The only consolation is she's going back to Russia, right?"

Augustine nodded. "She could seek asylum or file for citizenship, but she would need an immigration attorney."

"He wouldn't dare."

"Help her file and pay for an attorney?"

"Yes."

He placed his hands gently on hers. "I hear she saved him from being murdered by the now dead Russian on the *Arisha*."

"Is she doing that just to perturb me?" Tessa tried to look away from the pair. "She's practically sitting on his lap. Wait, you don't think, she and he..."

Augustine met her gaze. "I wouldn't rule it out, but he was a prisoner on board." He paused. "I doubt it."

Tessa stared down at her tight fists on the table.

Commander Willis stood and headed toward them, leaving his investigative team to question Ray and Angelina. When he arrived, Agent Augustine stood and reached out to shake hands. "Please sit."

Willis stood next to the table. "As soon as my investigative team is done over there, they have some questions for you two."

"Thank you, Commander, for everything you've done."

"Agent, I will be glad when you're all off my ship. As far as your Agent Hamilton, I'll give my report with pending charges to Commander Chapman when we dock in Honolulu. It'll be up to him what happens from there."

Tessa pointed toward Ray and Angelina. "What happens with her?"

"Miss Nikitin has a valid visa, so she can stay in the US for up to six months, then she has to re-apply. Since she was crew on the *Arisha*, if the ship isn't here, she would probably face deportation. I did overhear she wants to seek asylum here."

"How long can that take?" she asked.

"I've heard up to five years," Willis responded.

She huffed. "Good. She can go back to Russia."

Willis raised his brow. "It could get complicated."

"What do you mean, complicated?"

"Miss Nikitin said she may be pregnant with Mr. Holland's child."

"What!" she screamed, standing. Augustine grabbed her arm and pulled her back down.

Commander Willis scowled. "You see, this is why I want you all off my ship. I feel for all involved, but this falls under someone else's jurisdictions." He turned and walked back to the other table.

"Does what I said before make more sense now?" Augustine asked.

"What?"

"You don't know their circumstances, nor does Ray know of yours. I tell you what, I'll take Miss Nikitin aside so you and Ray can talk as soon as the investigative team is through. We still have time before we dock in Honolulu."

Tessa was uncertain what to say, nervous about her response to whatever Ray had to say. Unsure which way this would go. She glared at the agent, looked back at Ray twice, drooping her head, then agreed. The investigative team finished up a short time later after only asking a few questions of Agent Augustine and Tessa. Augustine left their table and sat with Ray and Angelina.

After a few minutes, Ray stood and came to sit across from Tessa.

"Tessa, I was a dead man. Beaten, crawling around on a rusty ship, being taken to Russia to die."

"Stop," she said.

"No, you need to hear this."

"Stop. I have something to tell you. I may be pregnant also."

Ray glared for a long moment before Tessa went on to explain Agent Hamilton, her drinking, what she awoke to, and the hospital examination results. Ray stayed silent through the entire explanation. When she finished, a chuckle rose from his throat and evolved into choking laughter, which quickly turned to sobs. He stood up, walked around the table, hugged, and kissed Tessa. They swayed back and forth in a strong embrace like they were dancing.

#

At the other table, Angelina wept.

Augustine said, "It's better this way, Angelina. Together, they can help you, apart it would never work out."

"You don't understand, I can't go back to Russia."

"I don't see that happening. Love them both, and they'll take care of you."

Angelina stood, tears running down her cheeks. She wiped them with her bandaged hand as she shuffled over to the embraced pair. They stopped and glanced at her, as she reached out her arms and moved close to hug them both. The trio held each other for long moments.

Agent Augustine smiled, observing from the distant table.

Epilogue

Two weeks later, the *Arisha*, having undergone repairs for her cooling issues, was cleared to leave port with her crew. No formal charges were made against the crew or captain. After being strongly encouraged by the Port State Control and US Coast Guard, the crew members were overjoyed to finally receive their paychecks from Dimitri Mishkin's shipping company, enabling the ship's release from the port hold. Vladislav's body was released to Captain Semenov after a formal autopsy. First officer Leonid Kotov and Denis Elin were not on board when the *Arisha* left port and were considered deserters.

After Ray, Tessa, and Angelina checked into a single room at the Waikiki Beach Marriott Resort, Ray called his mother. She was sober and relieved to hear he and Tessa were okay. David's memorial had been the day prior at Alta Mesa Memorial Park. The pastor's wife had been helping her cope with the changes. She told Ray she was eager for him to return home and take over for the pastor's wife.

Whenever the woman was there, Ray's mom kept misplacing her wine glass.

Since none of the three had ever vacationed in Hawaii, they stayed two weeks. First order of business was shopping for clothing for the tropical temperatures. Tessa was relieved to have Angelina dressed in more than just a T-shirt after the first couple of days in the hotel room. Angelina was glad to have a hat and gloves to stop people from glaring at her ear and missing finger. But she eventually gave up the gloves, which had created more stares and questions in the warm climate. Three days after docking, the Coast Guard released possession of Ray's remaining GG devices, components, and stones from the *Arisha*.

Together in the hotel room, Ray and Tessa packaged the components individually and arranged shipment to their Palo Alto home. The rest of their time they spent in a variety of lounges and lying on the beach. After getting to know Angelina better, Tessa began helping her with her English.

Agent Augustine met them for coffee two days before their planned return to Palo Alto, letting them know about Agent Hamilton. He was not terminated from the FBI, but reassigned to desk work at Quantico, far away from Tessa. Hamilton's sister, Augustine's wife, signed him up, without objection, with a sexual abuse therapist twice a week to start. He still claimed he did nothing wrong.

# # #

After arriving home in Palo Alto, Angelina and Tessa made quick work of cleaning up the disaster of clothes and cosmetics strewn about, thanks to Angelina's organizational skills. Tessa was so impressed, she set up a spare bedroom for Angelina to stay. They helped her with an application to enroll at Stanford University and would pay all the costs.

Ray waited to make a decision about going back to work at Laubner Labs until his foot was fully healed. He also wanted to see if he still felt comfortable there after his father's passing, as his dad had played a part in helping him secure his engineer position. Regardless of his return to Laubner Labs, he wanted more information about the circumstances that led up to his father's heart attack, and the words of the chief operating officer, but that would have to wait. Meanwhile, he thoroughly enjoyed being pampered by the two lovely young women who lived with him in his home.